Letting go

Ian Searle

Copyright © 2024 Ian Searle

All rights reserved. No part of this publication may be reproduced or transmitted in any form or by any means, electronic or mechanical including photocopying, recording or any information storage or retrieval system, without prior permission in writing from the publishers.

The right of Ian Searle to be identified as the author of this work has been asserted by him in accordance with the Copyright, Designs and Patents Act 1988

First published in the United Kingdom in 2024 by

The Cloister House Press

ISBN 978-1-913460-79-2

Chapter one

The car came to a halt at the front door. Frank looked at the old house as though for the first time. The word home no longer felt appropriate. This was a large, handsome building into which he and Louise had poured effort and love for thirty years. Her death had changed many things. His emotions were like the tiny particles of artificial snow in a paperweight which had been given a sudden, vigorous shaking. They still whirled and danced, refusing to settle. He felt almost numb, but some of the coruscating particles provoked sudden, sharp, and unexpected pain.

Poppy watched anxiously as her father took the few steps to the door and fumbled with the key. He looked all at once like an older man although she knew he was a little over sixty. She followed him in. They headed for the kitchen diner where Frank sat gratefully at the table while his daughter made a pot of tea.

"I'm sorry about the shambles at the wake," he said.

"It wasn't a shambles," she said. "And you need hardly apologise. You've just lost your wife."

Even these few words choked in her throat. She had lost her mother.

"I always think that paying your respects is a strange expression. There must have been, what, forty or fifty people there, all people who thought a lot of your mother. But the room was full of gossip and laughter."

"It's exactly what Mummy would have wanted. It wasn't a time, it isn't a time to mope and be so miserable, even if that seems more natural. It's a time to remember the good things. That's what the wake is for."

"I suppose you're right. I'm just not ready for that yet. Nor were George and Ann. Maybe wakes are for the young. They were keen to get away after the service."

"They seemed older," said Poppy. She was very fond of her grandparents, but she had never thought of them as old. Their daughter's death had hit them hard.

"Daddy," she said unexpectedly, "when did you last eat?"

He looked surprised by this. "I had a sandwich yesterday lunchtime," he said, "and sausage rolls at the hotel this afternoon."

"And when did you have a hot meal?"

"I don't remember."

Poppy walked over to the fridge. Without more ado she began to cook bacon and eggs. He watched her, mildly interested. He had not really felt hungry since Louise had died. He had been at a loss in every sense. The GP had been helpful. The undertaker had been more so. The vicar had done his best to console him, but it had felt like empty words. It was only when Poppy had arrived three days earlier that he began to come back to life. It was a very painful process. It was only ten weeks since Louise had been diagnosed with pancreatic cancer, a sentence of death which Frank felt was for him as well as for his wife. The illness was short and painful, although the doctors and nurses had done their best to make it less so. When, at last, Louise had died, he felt that he was like an empty husk of some great, tough-skinned gourd which had been invaded by a huge, hungry caterpillar. It had eaten him away from the inside, in the course of his work he had seen many such fruits which had been similarly eaten, with only the small hole left to show where the grub had entered or left.

He ate the food dutifully together with a piece of bread and then he drank a cup of tea.

"While I think about it," he said, "your mother wanted you to have the bits and pieces of jewellery. If you come up to the bedroom with me, I'll dig them out for you."

Poppy followed him up the stairs. She felt mildly uncomfortable in the bedroom, this intimate space where her parents had known each other in ways she could only imagine and which she preferred not to. Frank pointed to the dressing room stool where she sat as he found the jewellery box and put it on the table in front of her before sitting on the edge of the bed. She opened it. Her mother had good taste. Most of the pieces were costume jewellery and Poppy remembered seeing her mother wear them at various school functions. There were half a dozen rings, two of which she did not recognise. They had been her grandmother's, Frank told her.

"Don't forget to take them all with you, when you go," he said. "I only want to hang onto the mirror and hairbrush."

They made their way back downstairs.

"What are you planning to do?" Poppy asked. "I imagine you will be going back to work."

"No," he said. "I've been told they will keep the job open for me for up to a year, and I'm going to hold them to that. It's what we planned, even though the circumstances have changed."

"You think that's a good idea? Don't you think it would be better for you to have something to occupy yourself? You can't go on mourning for ever."

"I think you're wrong about that," he said, "but we won't argue about it. And I'm not going to be sitting around idle for the next twelve months. I have plans."

"What plans?"

"We had been saving, your mother and I, for the past three years and more. She was going to take retirement before she fell ill and we were going to do something we had both wanted to do for years – travel. We wanted to travel right across Canada by train. We also wanted to go cruising and whale watching. If there was enough money by then we would have wanted to visit the Antarctic. We had saved quite a lot of money for that."

"So, you are going cruising?"

"No, I don't want to go on my own. Without Louise it would not be the same."

"So, what are you planning to do?"

"I'm going back to my roots," he said.

"Your roots? And where are they? I don't think I've ever heard you talk about your past or your family. I know a little bit about Mummy's family, but nothing at all about yours."

"I don't know very much about it myself. And I haven't ever talked about it because I don't know anything. I can only remember bits of my childhood."

"I think Mummy once said that you had been brought up by an aunt, not by your own mother."

"That's true, Aunt Betty. It wasn't a very happy childhood. Her husband was much older than her and she was more than twenty years older than me. She didn't like me. I think she probably resented me."

"What became of her? Are you still in touch?"

"I left school early and started work at the age of fifteen. Two years after that I moved out of my aunt's house. We didn't keep in touch and I have no idea what happened to her. If she is still alive, she must be getting on for ninety now."

And you're going back to trace her whereabouts?"

"In part, yes. But I also want to find out about my mother."

"What happened to her?"

"All I know is that she died when I was three years old."

"So, you never knew her?"

"I never knew her and I don't know how she died."

"Well, it sounds like a mystery but it also sounds pretty gloomy. Are you sure this is a good idea?"

"Yes. It will give me a purpose and God knows I need a purpose at the moment. You can't possibly understand what the loss of your mother means. She was my reason for living."

"Oh, Daddy!" Poppy moved over to hug her father.

Poppy had to return to her job at the end of the week. She remained concerned about her father's mental health. It was obvious that the loss of his wife had robbed him of more than a companion and lover. Louise had always been full of vitality and energy. In her every day relationships she was positive and cheerful. The children in the school where she was the headmistress regarded her with affection and not a little awe as someone full of ideas. Occasionally her colleagues found her almost too stimulating and demanding, but they appreciated the energy and initiative she showed at every step of the way.

It was extraordinary that she and Frank had found each other. They were different both in temperament and in interests. Their first meeting had been when Frank, already the

Deputy Head Gardener for the Borough, had been inspecting one of the flower beds in the park. The flowers did not seem to be doing as well as he had expected so, at 7 o'clock on this morning he was kneeling to dig up one plant as a sample. He placed it in a plastic bag and then filled bottle with some soil before stepping back. Louise, on her normal, morning run, could not avoid him and they both ended up sprawled on the grass verge. Neither was seriously hurt. In the conversation which followed Louise explained that she was planning to establish a small garden at the primary school where she was an assistant teacher. She asked Frank for advice. He was happy to oblige, and he continued to help her with the project. They discovered interests in common – music, films, gardening. Frank was particularly knowledgeable about plants, not only those cultivated under his care, but also wild plants. He and Louise made one or two excursions into the countryside as well as to large gardens. Frank was by nature a shy, retiring man, unlike Louise, who was at ease in parties and official gatherings. When she gained promotion and eventually became the Headmistress, she was very happy in the role. Frank was content to watch her from a distance for some time.

Louise's ease in company came partly from her upbringing and childhood. When she persuaded him to meet her parents for the first time, Frank was nervous and awkward. Louise's father was a successful surgeon, self-assured, accustomed to making decisions. His wife, Ann, was equally self-assured, established in her own social circle, ready to help with the administration of local charities, to attend formal events with her husband. They both found their daughter's friend unprepossessing. At first relations between them were strained. They appeared to see Frank like the gamekeeper, Lady Chatterley's Lover. Louise worked hard to change their minds. Fortunately, they trusted her judgement so, when Louise told them firmly that she intended to marry Frank, enumerating his virtues of industry, skill, trustworthiness, and reliability, they gave the couple their full support.

The most obvious evidence of such support was financial help. Neither Louise nor Frank had a great deal of money, so they hoped to find somewhere to rent. George insisted that he would give them as a wedding present the deposit on a house. Such generosity was embarrassing for Frank, who would have refused it, but Louise was happy to accept. For a long time, it remained a source of embarrassment. An old farmhouse on the outskirts of the Borough became available. It was run down and in need of refurbishment, but there was a large piece of land which Frank knew would make a great garden, once the entire house had been redecorated. A timely promotion for both Frank and Louise, meant they would manage the mortgage. George's offer secured this house and for the next year and more the two young people spent long hours on the work. George was impressed, when he and Ann accepted the invitation to inspect.

"For a gardener," he told Frank, "You make a good builder and decorator. You must have doubled the value of this place. The garden is going to give you trouble, though."

The were standing at the window of the conservatory.

"Oh, the garden's the easy bit," Frank said.

George looked at him, but saw that he was stating the truth as he saw it. Indeed, borrowing equipment from work, Frank cleared the site in a matter of two weeks, revealing what he described as 'a blank canvas'. He and Louise spent many hours designing the garden, with fruit trees and a productive vegetable plot at the far end, and an area of lawn for their children to enjoy. They both wanted a big family to make good use of this large property, inside and out. At each step of the reclamation of both house and garden George's respect and admiration for his son-in-law grew. With the birth of their granddaughter there came a radical change as Frank grew steadily more self-assured.

The marriage surprised most of Louise's friends, but it proved a very successful one. Poppy was born two years into the marriage. It was a difficult birth as a result of which Louise was unable to have more children. The young couple refused to allow the end of their plans to trump the joy of the new arrival.

"It's sad," Frank said, "but, if we are destined to have only one child, it's going to be the best child ever."

They both loved Poppy but were determined not to spoil her. She was indeed a joy, making friends, quick to learn, popular like her mother. Temperamentally, Frank had learned over the years to view life and nature as it were through the twin lenses of conflict and decay. The journey he was about to undertake now was destined to modify this vision, although he did not know it. The combined effects of Louise and Poppy had already challenged his perceptions. They gave him constant joy.

Impatient to get away, once Poppy had returned to her work with urgent, repeated requests that he keep in close contact, Frank lost no time in making the necessary arrangements. His neighbours, Jack, and Iris, were happy to look after his house, drawing the curtains and switching on the lights every evening, feeding the cat, watering the garden. Three days after Poppy left, he packed a suitcase, his laptop, and his mobile phone, and set off. He drove steadily eastward. His mind was blank. His eyes took in the scenery but it aroused no interest. He felt no emotion. It was as though his brain was numb. He stopped twice when his body reminded him that he was hungry, but he had no idea where he stopped until he was within a mile or two of his destination. Memories flickered. It was many years since he had lived in Oakmere. A group of five trees on a small hill seemed familiar. He did not fully recognise the road, trusting to his satnav, but the trees, the hedges, the vegetation, even the weeds reminded him of the soil in which they grew. At last, he reached the main street of the little town. He approached from the north end. Although the road had been straightened and widened, he recognised the bridge and almost immediately the High Street. His old Grammar School passed by on the right. Fifty yards on the left he reached the Farmers' Arms and turned into the arched coachway. He made his way to Reception. He was disappointed. One of his most earnest ambitions as a boy had been to stay in this hotel. Now it looked shabby. He checked in, sent Poppy a text, then went downstairs, where a middle-aged bartender made him a pot of tea. He sat in a large, leather chair and gazed around.

The place was indeed shabby but clean. On a table there was a collection of newspapers, including the local paper, its logo unchanged after all these years. He took it to his chair and browsed. He appeared to be the only guest, but it was only late afternoon. Perhaps the public bar might get busier as the locals drifted in from work.

He finished his tea and stepped out into the street. He recognised the street layout, even the little Barclays next door to the equally small Boots. Not surprisingly, however, many of the small shops had changed or disappeared altogether. And he was sure there had been a small cinema almost opposite the Farmers' Arms. It was now a supermarket. He walked back to the Grammar School. He would explore that another day perhaps. There had once been a large tree in the very front, growing out of the cobbles. That had gone. From the main road he could see the old Hall, a dignified building in sandstone. That had not changed either, but he did not recognise the buildings beyond it. Opposite the Hall was the jumble of Edwardian buildings that had formed the residential part of the school. Here several of the teachers, including the Headmaster and his wife, had their accommodation and about one hundred boarders lived. With that memory came that of food and an image of the dark dining hall with its bare, polished tables and long benches. Frank had never been a boarder; he had only attended the school for three years until his aunt and uncle had insisted, he left.

This was part of his life which he had virtually buried. He had left this little town at the age of seventeen and had never returned. Until now he had been happy to forget it. But he could not explain to himself why or how he had experienced the recent compulsion to return. He had told Poppy he was exploring his roots. As a professional gardener, that was exactly how he viewed this quest. He was unearthing the past in order to understand better how he had grown into the man he was. He suspected that those roots had been subject to attack. Maybe they were malformed. He was certain they were not entirely healthy. He turned and made his way back to the Farmers' Arms.

There was no dining room, but traditional, pub meals were served in the bar. He entered the public bar and ordered scampi and chips. The beer, a real ale which the barman recommended, was surprisingly good and he sat at the bar to wait for his meal. As he had suspected this is where local customers came. Three men came in together, nodded to him, ordered drinks, and took them to a large table at the back of the room. By the time his meal was ready, the group of drinkers had grown, all male, all apparently regulars. They formed a large, friendly group, chatting. Frank ate his scampi, and was grateful for the bottled sauce. He ordered another pint. One of the drinkers came to the bar to order a new round.

"On holiday?" he asked. "We don't get very many visitors."

"Yes, just for a few days. I used to live here years ago as a child."

"Well, you look sad and lonely on your own at the bar. Come and join us"

"I can't barge in on your club meeting."

"It's not a club. Well, I suppose it could be called a club. It just sort of developed over the years. Some men have men's sheds I believe. We just agreed to meet here once a week for a pint or two. Come and join us."

Frank found himself following Steve, as he introduced himself, to the head of the table, where he was ushered into a large Windsor chair. "We always keep it empty," Steve explained, "just in case there is an unexpected guest like yourself."

All eyes were on Frank.

"Everybody, this is Frank," Steve announced. "And this motley collection," he said, indicating the friendly faces," consists of Phil, John, Mike, Porky." Porky was as tall and thin as a beanpole. Frank looked puzzled. "Ah," Steve continued, "Porky breeds pigs, hence the nickname. Next to him there is Colin, then the Doc, then Primrose." Nothing could have been less appropriate, Frank thought. The man called Primrose had the face of a prize fighter. The flesh was puffy and wrinkled. The nose had clearly been broken more than once. Either side dark eyes gleamed under heavy brows. The man held up a huge hand and answered Frank's unspoken question. "Don't ask," he said, "just don't ask." Frank was never to learn the answer. He was already beginning to feel the effects of the two pints he had drunk unwisely. He rarely drank at all and he found it impossible to remember the names. "Richard, Gordon, Mac and Pat," Steve concluded the introductions.

"And where are you from?" one of the men asked.

"I live in Berkshire these days," Frank began.

"Far, far away in a distant galaxy," someone else said.

"So, what brings you all this way to this, the dead centre of the universe?"

"I just wanted to see how the place had changed," he said.

There was a laugh from the far end of the table. "Nothing ever changes here."

"Well, the cinema has gone. It's now a supermarket, I see."

"The cinema?" one of the younger men asked. "That was a cinema?"

"The Gaumont."

"Well, I never!"

"It looks as though the old Grammar School has also changed," said Frank.

"Oh, that was a long time ago, it must be, what, forty years?"

"Really?"

"At least that long. If you can remember that far back," it was a small, balding man of uncertain age who spoke. "You may remember there was a Secondary Modern school next door to it, brand-new in the fifties."

"Oh, yes," I remember that being built."

"Well, they decided to amalgamate the two schools on the new site. It doesn't look very new these days, all plate glass and plastic, but the Grammar School closed and the buildings were sold off. They look much the same from the outside, but the main part, the old Victorian or Edwardian buildings, the good-looking part, was converted into private flats and apartments."

"Good heavens! I thought you said nothing changed. That was a big change surely."

This provoked some quiet discussion which was brought to an abrupt end when Frank suddenly stood up, knocking the chair back behind him. He turned away from the table and made a hasty, undignified exit towards the toilets on the other side of the room. The alcohol made him unsteady, and he did not so much walk as stagger as quickly as he could. Everyone was startled. Steve, realising that all was not well, followed Frank just as he disappeared through the door of the Gents. Frank just made it and within seconds was being violently sick. When at last he straightened up, his face was white and clammy with sweat. He was highly embarrassed but grateful for Steve's helping hand as he dashed water on his face and pulled down the roller towel to dab it dry.

"I'm sorry," he said.

"What were you drinking?" Steve asked.

"Something called Eagle's Blood, I think. The barman recommended it. Real ale, he said, brewed locally."

"It's lethal," Steve said, "something like 8%."

"Sorry to ruin your evening," Frank said," but I think I need to lie down."

Steve insisted on seeing him back to his room. Frank was clearly badly affected and had to cling to the banister all the way to the top of the staircase. He got inside, filled the tooth glass with cold water and drank it down, clung on grimly to the little wash basin while he cleaned his teeth, staggered as far as the bed and let himself fall, kicking off his shoes to lie otherwise fully clad while the room continued to revolve around him.

When he woke up it was completely dark. His head was pounding, his mouth horribly dry, and his ribs ached. He sat on the edge of the bed and looked at his watch, 2:30 am. He pulled the curtains and turned on the light before undressing and taking a shower. He felt a little better, dressed in clean pyjamas. Surprisingly, he felt hungry. He made himself a cup of tea and ate two of the little packets of biscuits before crawling under the duvet and turning off the light.

"Tea!" Frank became aware that someone was talking to him. He opened his eyes and winced as the light hit him.

"Thought you might like a pot of tea and some biscuits," said the voice. Frank struggled to consciousness, thanked the man who brought the tea, and checked the time. It was 7:45. He poured the tea with hands that were shaking. He would have preferred to be left to sleep it off, but the hot drink was certainly welcome. He poured himself a second cup but, before he had time to drink it, someone tapped on the door and came in. He was about to say that he wanted to be left alone when he recognised the figure that came in as Doc, one of the people at the party. What, he wondered, was going on.

"You are probably feeling awful," said Doc. "I have a surgery in half an hour, but I thought I'd look in quickly to see if you were okay. I recommend plenty of fluids, eat a decent breakfast, and take it easy for the morning. Is there anything I can do for you otherwise?"

"I don't think I have any painkillers," said Frank. "But it's very kind of you to call in, thank you very much, over and beyond the call of duty, I think they call this."

"We all feel a bit responsible," said Doc. "We had a pretty stiff talk to Jeremy."

"Jeremy?"

"The bartender. He should have known better than to serve you that foul beer."

"It tasted good."

"It may do, but it was toxic. It's not a good idea to poison your guests on the first night." He had retrieved a small bottle of paracetamol which he handed to Frank. "Don't forget, a decent breakfast. You may not think you need it, but you do. My surgery is only two doors down, should you need it."

An hour later, having eaten a poached egg on toast, Frank left for a walk round the town. He walked briskly to the top of the small hill where the parish church stood. He was not especially interested in churches but this was a convenient place to pause. The bright sunlight was still quite irksome. Inside there was the usual faint smell of incense. It was not a large church, but large enough to accommodate two aisles. He took a few steps down the right- hand aisle. It must be on the south side, he calculated. He sat in the cool half-light and a distant memory came to him of having been here before. It must have been when he was twelve years old. There was some special anniversary to do with the foundation of the school. The entire school had been marshalled in the playground by the staff. There had been an inspection parade. All the boys had to be wearing a cap, a blazer, and the school tie. All the teachers wore their gowns. Most of them were plain, black things like blackout curtains, but the woman who taught music had blue and yellow, and the headmaster wore a hood trimmed with white fur, ermine, he was told. Two by two, the entire school had wound its way through the streets of the town up to this church for the special service. Frank remembered nothing of the service itself other than tedium. Afterwards there had been half day holiday.

The old chemist's shop was still nearby. Frank purchased a pair of sunglasses before resuming his walk. He turned into a side road, which took him into a small, wooded area, winding paths lead up and around the hill and on the other side they sloped down to the banks of the river. This was the same river that he had crossed when entering the town. Here, however there was no traffic. There were numerous birds and the steady sound of running water. It was exactly the kind of peaceful place he loved. There was even a convenient bench. He sat and rested for a long time. Despite the traces of discomfort from the previous evening, he felt more at ease than at any time since Louise's death.

He walked back into town and found a café where he drank coffee. All morning he had been putting off time to visit Barrett Street. He was not compelled to do so but he would regret it if he did not. It was a road lined with residential housing, rundown like much of the rest of the town. He steeled himself to walk its entire length. Halfway down on the left was the short terrace of five houses. Unlike the other buildings these were built on three stories. The front doors looked dusty and tired, as did the windows, but they were serviceable housing stock. He stood opposite number 15 and stared at it for a while. The bow window on the ground floor was screened with lace curtains. In his mind he was recalling the layout of the three floors, including the small bedroom at the back which had been his for seventeen dismal years. After such a long time he was glad to realise that he no longer felt the same kind of dismay. He turned back and took another side road which was clearly labelled Orchard Street. Earlier he had glimpsed a modern inn sign which he now tracked down. Unlike the Farmers' Arms, this little establishment looked clean and tidy. The owners had decorated it with window boxes. Frank stopped for a moment to consult the menu which was pinned beneath the sheet of glass outside. It did not offer haute cuisine, but looked a little more inviting. He went in. There were four small dining tables in the bar, two of them occupied by couples. The bartender smiled at him and a young woman, who was preparing meals in full view of the customers also smiled a greeting. He ordered the smoked mackerel and salad together with bottled water.

Afterwards he stepped out into the street again and was greeted by name by a man in working clothes. "Hello again, Frank! How are you feeling today?" It was one of the party from the previous evening, Gordon.

"Tell me," Frank said, "there's something familiar about this street, but I can't make it out. Has it changed a great deal?"

"The pub is quite new," Gordon explained, "but the rest is much the same. The second- hand shop over there has been here as long as I can remember."

"Maybe that's it," Frank said. "I'm sorry for spoiling your evening last night."

Gordon laughed. "I wouldn't put it like that," he said. "I expect we shall be talking about it for weeks to come. But Jeremy was very naughty, selling you that awful beer."

"I'm strictly teetotal today," said Frank, and the two men parted company. It was only a few steps to the second-hand shop. He prodded some of the clothes hanging on a rack outside the door and peered into the dusty windows but was not tempted inside. He was realising why the place was familiar. This had been his uncle's shop. He looked up at the fascia board, half expecting to see the name in faded paint, Kristinin. He had not found the name particularly strange, since he had grown up with it. They had never adopted him, so he retained his mother's name, Whitaker. Now he was glad of the fact. It was the only thing his mother had left him, other than half his genes. Kristinin, whatever his origins, had earned a living of sorts as a pawnbroker. The name had long since gone but there was still a rusty mark where the pawnbrokers' sign had hung over the pavement.

He left Orchard Street and headed back as far as the public library. It was only a modest branch, staffed by one bespectacled lady. Frank asked if he could use the computer. She was quite surprised, telling him there was a charge of one pound per hour. He spent the hour in a fruitless search for any records of his mother. Then he paid his dues and asked where the Registry Office was. It was tucked round the corner in a building he did not remember, a large building of stone. He pushed open the door. He was in a corridor that smelled of floor polish and bleach. Overhead there was a staircase and signage which told him that there was a major room for ceremonies upstairs. Immediately on his right a wooden notice projected from a wall with the word "Reception" printed on it. Underneath the sign there was a window and a counter. His enquiries here were also fruitless, although the Registrar explained that all records were now held centrally in Guildford, twenty-five miles away. Frank gave up for the day. He was in any case beginning to feel tired again. He called into the supermarket and bought some basic food supplies to take back to his room.

He took advantage of the bar to drink more tea. His phone pinged. He flipped it open to see a sun-filled photograph of white buildings and a pure, blue sea beyond. The text read only "CU soon. P XXX". He smiled. Later he spent several hours watching documentaries in his bedroom. He made himself a simple snack and went to bed early.

Chapter two

Armed with the full name and the year of his mother's death, it proved remarkably easy to obtain a copy of the death certificate the following day. He was asked to wait a while. He killed time window shopping. He returned, paid the fee, and was given an A4 envelope which he took to a nearby café. He sipped coffee and opened the envelope. The form reminded him inevitably of his wife's death certificate but he read it carefully. He did not expect a surprise, merely information about the cause of death. He was, therefore, startled to find that the cause was given as "Suicide while the balance of the mind was upset". It was a total shock. His mother had not been as much as twenty years old. What had driven her to take her own life? How had she done so? He had expected a straightforward piece of information. His Aunt Betty had simply told him that his mother had died when he was three years old. She had never elaborated and had left him to assume she had died of an illness. Why would a young mother abandoned her three-year-old son, leaving him in the care of her older sister? She must have been in a very bad state to do such a thing. He stared at the piece of paper in front of him, unable to comprehend. Instead of an answer to a question he was now faced by a deeply troubling mystery.

He walked for perhaps half an hour through unfamiliar streets, his mind in a whirl. He found himself at the entrance to a park. There was a bench nearby and he sat, trying to think things through. He had never needed Louise more than at this moment when she was no longer available. She would have been the one person he could talk to and receive understanding as well as advice. But there was no Louise any longer except in his memory. He tried to think logically how he could discover the truth about his mother's death. Reluctantly, he began to think about his Aunt Betty. She must know the circumstances. She would have been approaching thirty years old when her younger sister took her own life. She had never been keen to talk to her nephew about his mother or his origins. It was only when he had need of his own birth certificate that she had confirmed what the certificate showed, that no father had been registered. He was illegitimate. Frank had been made to feel that this was an indelible stain on his character, although he could not be held responsible for it. He had been conscious of the lack of a father at school and it had not been until he moved away at the age of seventeen to take up an apprenticeship that the feeling of inferiority had faded.

He had not spoken to or communicated with his aunt for over forty years. She would, in any case, now be aged nearly ninety. She may very well be dead or suffering from dementia. He had no idea how to track her down though that might be the only way he could discover the truth. He got up from the bench and walked back into town as another idea struck him. He visited a very large library. He asked the librarian if there were archives of local newspapers available. It was a long shot but it paid off. The Surrey and Southeast Chronicle produced a local weekly paper in numerous editions. The news and advertisements were the same for all editions, but several pages were given over to more local affairs, depending on the distribution. Frank was familiar with the newspaper, a copy of which he had seen in the Farmers Arms the previous day. The helpful librarian assisted his search on one of the computers, narrowing it to the relevant edition. He explained that he was looking for any reports about the suicide or inquest of a young girl, Madeleine Joyce Whitaker, in 1947. Settled in front of the computer, he began reading.

Much of what he read was of limited interest, being very local. There were brief reports of such sporting activities as village cricket or darts matches in the summer and occasional mention of parish council meetings. There was still a great deal to do with garden produce associations and competitions. It was still a time when food was rationed and the wartime exhortation to "Dig for Victory" was still in force. It would be four or five years before the last of the rationing came to an end, Frank remembered. There were reports from the local courts of various misdemeanours, the occasional pub brawl. There were also one or two obituaries. There was one small paragraph reporting the repatriation of a former Japanese prisoner of war whose health was quite fragile according to the writer. His diet had to be strictly controlled for several months until he regained sufficient strength to eat normally. There was one short article which caught his eye, announcing the appointment of two new teachers at the Grammar School. He recognised the names of two men. He learned that they had been invalided out of the army after being wounded and had returned to take up teaching posts which they had left. And finally, after searching for two hours, he found the headline, "Suicide of a young mother." Franks left the computer screen long enough to ask the friendly librarian for a sheet of paper and a pencil to take notes. Then he returned.

"Madeleine Joyce Whitaker, aged 19, took her own life while the balance of her mind was upset, the Coroner, Dr Willard Bothwell concluded at the end of his investigation today. Miss Whitaker and her young son, aged three years, were living with her sister and brother-in-law, a local businessman. The child will be cared for by his uncle and aunt. Ever since the birth of the son, Dr Bothwell said, Miss Whitaker had suffered deep and prolonged periods of depression. These had rendered her almost

incapable of taking care of her own child. She had been referred by her own doctor to the mental hospital where she was treated with antidepressant drugs, but there were plans afoot shortly to begin more radical treatment in the form of electroconvulsive therapy. Unfortunately, there was a delay before such treatment could begin. At 3 PM on May 5, 1947, Madeleine Whitaker had walked to the bridge over the railway on Westwood Road and had thrown herself off. She had landed on top of the small, tank engine and been thrown to one side with multiple injuries which must have been instantly fatal. A verdict of suicide while the balance of her mind was upset was duly recorded."

Frank copied this word for word and sat, stunned for a while before leaving.

"Are you all right?" The librarian was concerned. Frank realised he was, indeed, suffering from shock. He thanked her, paid the fees for the use of the computer, and left.

He was glad the Farmers Arms was not a popular drinking hole. He got back at about seven pm and sent a short text to Poppy before settling in the lounge. His thoughts were in a turmoil. He wanted to know more about his mother's suicide than the bare facts he had copied from the newspaper and the death certificate. He had not known his mother and had no memory of her. His aunt should surely have given him more information rather than mislead him. She must have been feeling ashamed, he concluded. That, if it was true, was no excuse for leaving him in the dark. Sitting in the shabby comfort of the old hotel, he though back to his childhood and the years he had spent in the house in Barret Street. He seldom thought about those times nor until he had undertaken this quest had he thought about Aunt Betty. At the age of 61 he now tried to remember the time before he had left, so many years previously.

He found it surprisingly difficult to remember Betty's face. She was a tall woman, broad shouldered and strong, that much he knew. She was strict to the point of being stern and he could remember no tenderness. His life was disciplined, arranged by the clock. To this day he found no trouble in getting up early, perhaps the only thing which would stand him in good stead. He still woke every morning at six. He had been expected to wash, dress and be downstairs for breakfast by 7 o'clock. Betty would inspect the back of his neck and behind his ears, making him show his teeth to prove he had cleaned them, and she checked he had polished his shoes ready for school, on school days. Immediately after breakfast he had chores to do. He could not remember her taking him to school, though she probably had taken him to his primary school. When he had passed the scholarship to the Grammar School, the result had not been celebrated, merely acknowledged as something to be expected, although he was not much of a scholar. He got by. When he came home in the afternoon, Betty made him a slice of bread, smeared with margarine and a thin layer of jam which he ate in the kitchen with a cup of tea. On school days he then went into the sitting room and sat at the cloth covered table to do his homework which she checked before allowing him to escape to his own room at the top of the house. For an hour he was free. He threw his schoolbag on the floor in an act of daring, but he always picked it up again later. He opened the window and looked out across the road towards the fields. At weekends and during the school holidays Betty found him plenty of household jobs to do, restricting his freedom, but he remembered glorious hours of freedom which he spent exploring the countryside only a matter of yards away from the familiar street. He could not remember anything resembling a family outing. His uncle whose image came back more readily, always dressed in black. He wore horn-rimmed glasses on a swarthy face and Frank had never seen him smile. His shop kept him busy from 9 o'clock in the morning until 6 o'clock in the evening. He seemed perpetually tired.

When Frank first went to the Grammar School, it was the first time that he was aware of some of the peculiarities that governed his own life. First there was the problem of names: he was registered as Frank Whitaker, although his uncle's name was Kristinin. He had no father, and he was cruelly bullied, called 'Little Bastard', or 'Jew-boy' out of the teachers' earshot. When obliged to change for games or PE, his classmates made a show of seeking to see if he had been circumcised. As for the teachers, they regarded him with indifference, since he was never terribly good at anything except botanical drawing. It was a skill he had little opportunity to show. He endured his four years in mute misery much of the time and was pitifully grateful to find work as a municipal gardener. He was paid thirty shillings a week. His aunt took one pound for his keep.

For the short time between leaving school and stumbling across the chance to apply for an apprenticeship many miles away, Fank had used his new-found freedom to wander the fields and woods and study plants, animals, and insects. His boss, one of the first kind people he had met, saw the boy had potential and was eager to know more about plants especially. He recommended signing up for evening classes. Frank was reluctant, given his experience at school, but during his first year, his attention drawn to an announcement in a trade paper by his horticultural friend, he applied for a residential apprenticeship in the town where he was to settle for the rest of his life. He could never believe his application had been successful

Betty's reaction had been disbelief at first. His decision to apply had occasioned no comment that Frank could now recall. When the job was confirmed, Betty was sceptical about his ability to succeed. He would join four other apprentices who would be accommodated in a small house with a resident Matron, the wife of the ambitious Head Gardener who would be responsible for their health and moral care. In this the couple were aided by the local vicar. To Frank, used not only to a loveless life, but one of long hours and hard work, this was freedom. The evening classes were replaced by day-release lessons one day a week, lessons which he enjoyed. He stood out among the five young men and acquired City and Guild Certificates and by the age of 23 he was a well-qualified gardener with papers to prove it. His aunt, when he looked back, had been diligent in checking the safeguards which went with the apprenticeship, but she was quite pleased to hand over responsibility. Although Frank had written to her dutifully once or twice, she had never replied.

Frank had grown used to his aunt's lack of emotional attachment and saw the move as entirely positive. Later he thought about his aunt's apparent relief to be shot of him. He remembered a cold atmosphere, his uncle's remote and stern face. It was not until he had left the household that he began to assign importance to minor incidents. In his own little room on the second floor, he sometimes heard raised voices from two floors down. Aunt and uncle showed no affection to each other nor to him. He did not know what the problems were, but they did not provide a warm home environment. Sometimes he wondered if he were the cause of the bad feeling, but if that was the case, neither his aunt nor his uncle gave any indication. He was treated always with indifference.

All these years later, faced with the revelation of his mother's suicide, he felt extremely frustrated at being unable to pursue his search for the truth. He now regretted having lost contact with his aunt who would surely have been able to provide some answers. He wondered if he could possibly track her down even now. He did not know where to begin and in any case, he did not even know if she was still alive. If she was alive, there was a real chance that she might have developed dementia, given her advanced age. It did not look very promising.

"Sorry to disturb you, sir." Frank opened his eyes. He must have been dozing.

"I'm closing the bar in five minutes," Jeremy explained. "Is there anything you want before I shut up shop?"

"Can you make me a pot of tea? I don't suppose you've got anything like sandwiches?"

"Tea is no problem. I haven't got any sandwiches I'm afraid. I'll see what I can rustle up."

Jeremy returned with the tea and some small, pre-wrapped pieces of cheese together with crackers. He also brought two packets of crisps. Frank thanked him. In the silent room he unwrapped the cheese which did not look very appetising, but he was hungry and ate it with the crackers and followed them with both packets of crisps. The salt left him feeling thirsty so he made his way up to his room and made yet more tea before going to bed.

Chapter three

After breakfast he walked briskly through the town, past the church, and back to the peaceful bench overlooking the river. It was a pleasant day. He sat and gazed at the water, listening to its gurgling and to the joyous sound of birds in the trees. Near the bank where the current was weak and interrupted by numerous small eddies, a family of moorhens paddled by. He watched them with affection. His head was still buzzing with confusion which, he realised, was akin to shock. Despite having no immediate memory of his mother, he felt surprisingly saddened by her death. He wanted to know what had driven her to such a point of desperation that she had deserted her own son and chosen a desperate and probably painful death for herself. He needed to know. He needed answers. There seemed to be no one who could provide them.

He walked back into town and headed for 15 Barrett Street and knocked on the door. After a few moments the door was opened by a woman who was clearly in the middle of cleaning the house. She pushed the vacuum cleaner to one side in the hallway.

"Can I help you?" she asked.

Frank explained that he was looking for the previous owners of the house, in particular Mrs Kristinin. He drew a blank. The new tenant shook her head. "Sorry," she said, "I've never heard of her. We bought the house from Mr and Mrs Williams."

Frank thanked her politely and walked back to Orchard Street, where he bought coffee and thought about his next move. Across the road from where he sat his eye lighted on the old shop. Without much hope he headed for it. Inside there was an extraordinary jumble. Along one wall were racks of clothing, similar to the ones outside. At the back of the room, which was quite large, there were bits of second-hand furniture. A three-piece suite, the chairs piled on top of the settee, was flanked by an old chest of drawers on one side and a dining table, scratched and poor, surmounted by four dining chairs. A large part of the room was furnished with tables upon which were displayed cardboard boxes full of oddments, from cutlery and kitchen utensils to second-hand books.

Frank browsed all this junk for a few minutes, watched by an elderly woman who sat behind a counter on the third wall of the room. She watched him closely, as though she suspected he might abscond with some of the goods. Instead, Frank turned to her and surprised her by asking how long she had owned the shop.

"I've been here thirty years," she said, suspicious.

"Goodness gracious! I'm sorry if I sound nosy," Frank said, "but the man that originally owned this place, a man called Vladimir Kristinin, was my uncle. May I ask if you bought it from him or had somebody else owned it?"

This information was of interest to the old lady. "Your uncle? Well, I I never! Yes, it was a pawn brokers in those days. I didn't want the hassle of lending money, not that I had much capital anyway. I had the three balls taken down and turned it into a second-hand shop, as you see."

"The fact is," Frank explained, "I completely lost track of my uncle. I'm trying to track him down."

"You won't have much luck with that," she said. "He died a few years later."

"What about his wife – his widow, my aunt?"

"Oh, I know nothing about that. In fact, I had very little to do with Mr Kristinin, even during the sale process. I just happened to see a notice of his death in the local paper sometime later."

"Oh, thank you anyway," Frank said, then, as a sudden thought struck him, "can I be so impertinent as to ask who did the conveyancing?"

"Good heavens! Well, I suppose there's no harm in my telling you. I assume you're not going to challenge my ownership; suggest you should have inherited it?"

Frank was startled at the very idea. "Of course not!" he said. "It's just that the solicitor may help me to trace my aunt. She used to live in Barrett Street."

"There wasn't much choice of solicitors in those days," said the shop owner. "Come to think of it, there can't be more than two or three solicitors in the town even now. I used the Blount and

Maggert firm. They're still working. It sounds like a fairly hopeless quest to me."

She could well be right, Frank thought as he walked back into the main streets. He found the offices of Blount and Maggot immediately. They were housed in a small, Victorian building of brick. He mounted the two steps in front of the heavy door and went in. A pretty young girl looked up from her computer screen and came to meet him.

"Can I help you?" she asked.

Frank tried to explain. The girl looked confused. "Would you like to take a seat?" she said, gesturing towards two chairs against the wall. Frank took a seat and the girl disappeared through an internal door. He did not have to wait very long. She had hardly time to give him a smile and resume her place behind their computer, when she was followed by a man. Frank stood up in astonishment as he recognised Steve, the man who had introduced him to what he thought of as the Men's Shed Group.

"Well, well, well," said Steve, holding out a hand in welcome. "Good to see you, Frank. Come into my office. I'll ask Maisie to bring us a cup of tea. Follow me."

Steve's office was on the ground floor. Its Victorian origins were still obvious – a small window, lots of dark wood, one wall given over entirely to shelves, loaded with beautifully bound, legal books. The desk was also antique and very large, but Steve took his place in a modern chair and waved Frank into one of two chairs facing him.

"Welcome to my kingdom," Steve said. "What is it I can do for you? Susan was not very clear."

Frank explained.

"You realise I can't give you any confidential information? Even if I can find records of the conveyancing of your uncle's shop, the documents will contain the personal information. I understand why you are trying to trace the present whereabouts of your aunt, but, even if I can find her, I cannot give you her personal details. The best I could do, always assuming we can track her down, is to ask her to contact me in the first instance and then, if she agrees yourself. And I'm afraid, even before we begin, I shall have to ask you for formal identification. I know we are looking back a good many years, but the regulations still apply."

Frank agreed these conditions were quite reasonable. He would, he said, return to the Farmers Arms where fortunately he had his passport. He didn't know why he had brought his passport on this trip, but was glad he had. He sipped his tea while Steve asked the girl called Maisie to search the archives which presumably were kept somewhere on the premises. This firm looked as if it had existed for decades. There would therefore be shelves or boxes full of papers gathering dust somewhere.

Steve seemed genuinely interested in Frank's search. He listened attentively to the story of Madeleine Whitaker's untimely death. He commented that things had changed radically since the 1940s, when it was a social taboo to have a child out of wedlock. In Madeleine's case the opprobrium would have been even worse because she was probably under age when she conceived. To date Frank had no clue as to who the father might be. Nowadays there was a far more liberal and tolerant attitude, thank goodness. In the case of Frank's mother, the resultant outrage, as her father had seen it, had driven the young teenager to seek the help of her sister, Betty. That she should have taken her own life three years later was a tragedy. He expressed his sympathy and understanding to Frank, whose childhood and early years had been so severely affected.

Maisie tapped on the door and came in. She was clutching a small bundle of papers which were tied up with red tape. She handed the bundle to Steve.

"Well," he said, "at least we have the records of the conveyancing. I shall now peruse these and wait for you to come back with the documentary proof that you have a rightful interest. I hope we can find out something useful for you, though I am far from sure we shall."

Frank returned with his passport in half an hour. With his permission, Steve photo copied the relevant pages and handed it back to him.

"Leave it with me now," he said. "I'll do my research, but it will take a little while. I don't know if there will be any record here of where your aunt went once the probate on your uncles will had been sorted. I'll see what I can do. If I can find a forwarding address of any kind, I shall contact her to seek her permission before giving you the information. I hope that is clear."

It was at least a chance. Frank thanks Steve for his help and spent the rest of the day on a long walk in the countryside, trying to remember the tracks and pathways he had explored as a child. It was an altogether enjoyable experience, especially when he found an area of woodland which he had almost forgotten. He used his mobile phone to take a lot of photographs of the flora. The underlying geology here was quite different from that of his adopted area. This was the Weald, the farmland on the northern side of the South Downs. Here there was a great deal of clay. A small stream ran through the wood, a clear stream, the origin of which was a spring, no more than two miles away. Water on the grassy, chalk uplands drained through to produce sparkling, clear water. Even here it was still unpolluted, despite the use of agricultural chemicals on the surrounding fields. It was, thought Frank, like a pure oasis.

He strode back to the Farmers Arms late in the afternoon. The exercise was good for him, but it left him very tired. He ate another unimaginative meal in the bar before taking himself off to his bedroom. Poppy sent him a short text. He replied. Her words made him think once more about Louise and he was plunged unexpectedly into grief for a while. He roused himself, splashed cold water on his face, made himself a hot drink, then watched documentaries on the small television screen.

There was nothing much he could do the following day except wait. He could hardly expect any news from Steve yet. In fact, he was reconciled to having to wait at least a week. That was probably ambitious. He was at something of a loose end as he wandered down the main street. A large, green, double-decker bus rolled towards and past him . The destinations shown on the front were all familiar but one in particular made him stop for a moment. A woman who was walking past with her shopping bags very nearly ran into him. He apologised.

She gave him a curious look and walked on. What had caught his eye was the name of a village, Larch. Larch was the village where his mother, Madeleine, had been born, the village, presumably, where he had been conceived. It was also the village where his grandparents had lived. They would surely both be dead by now. Betty, their eldest daughter, was approaching ninety after all. They would have known the truth.

He enquired at the newsagents at the bottom of the street when the next bus would be going to Larch. It was, he was told, an hourly service in each direction. He decided to leave his car at the pub and take the bus out there. It was only three miles away. He had no idea what he hoped to find after all this time. He did not expect to gather any useful information, but it would be a pleasant way of passing the time.

Larch was a simple village. It consisted almost entirely of one street with houses on either side, most of them with generous gardens. At one end of the street there was a pub, the Six Blackbirds, and at the other end, the small church, hidden discreetly from the pub by the curve of the road. Small lanes led left and right led into the countryside. Frank ignored the pub and headed as far as the church. He had no great interest in ecclesiastical buildings, but there was little else of note to look at. The houses which lined the road provided a curious mixture of redbrick Victoriana and one or two more modern designs. It was quite pleasing to look at. The side streets were little more than lanes which he explored briefly as he made his way to the church. The buildings petered out as they seemed to lose contact with the main street.

The church had the usual, musty smell. It was quite small. As he opened the heavy door, he was obliged to step down a few inches onto the rough, flagstone floor. There was not a great deal to see. There was some Victorian glass in one window, and one or two memorial plaques. Frank emerged into the open air, thinking the churchyard might be more interesting. He wandered, reading the inscriptions on the headstones for a few minutes, then took a seat on a conveniently placed wooden bench. The land fell away towards the bottom of the graveyard. To his left was the church, beyond which there were three mature yew trees. Beyond the boundary wall was a large, sloping meadow in which a small herd of cows munched its way, hardly moving.

"Do you mind if I sit down?" An elderly man, walking slowly with the aid of two sticks appeared from the tarmac path behind him.

"Of course not," said Frank.

The older man sat carefully and leaned his two sticks in the corner. This was obviously something he did habitually. He was wearing an almost threadbare black suit. Not only was it shiny with age, the elbows looked very close to turning into holes. He wore a dog collar.

"What do you think of our little church?" he asked.

"Very cosy – comforting," said Frank.

"Parts of it are Saxon, you know."

"Really? I don't know much about architecture."

"What brings you here to Larch? I've not seen you here before that I remember."

"I'm revisiting my childhood," Frank explained. "I was actually born and brought up in Oakmere, but my grandparents lived here in Larch."

At this the old priest perked up. "Your grandparents? What was the name?"

"Whitaker."

Thes interest was immediately stimulated. "Whitaker?" he repeated.

"Yes, that was a long time ago. They must be dead by now. I'm sixty-one, after all."

The old man was studying him. "Forgive me for asking," he said, "but what was your mother's maiden name? I assume she would be a Whitaker. I have lived in Larch all my life, you see. I was living here when you were born. I was a young man, of course, but I do remember something of the troubles surrounding your grandparents."

"You remember? That's really why I came here. You see, I was born in Oakmere. My mother's name was Madeleine. I hardly knew her. I certainly don't remember her, and I have just learned that I was an illegitimate child and that my mother took her own life."

"My dear boy! How terrible for you!"

"I am very keen to find out more," Frank said, "so, anything you can tell me, I would be very grateful."

The priest gave his name as Father Bernard Kerswell. He told Frank what he knew of the tragic events many years previously. Young Madeleine had been thrown out of her home in disgrace. She was pregnant and beginning to show. Her parents, Frank's grandparents, had been not only shocked, but they had also been unforgiving. Rumour had it that, when quizzed unmercifully by her father, she had refused to reveal the name of the child's father but had claimed that she had been raped. She was not believed. Thus, it was that she had thrown herself on the mercy of her older sister, Betty.

"Raped!" This was a new element in the story. If it was true, then Frank's mother had been even more badly treated and wronged. He wondered if the alleged rape, or the fact that nobody would believe her, had anything to do with the "disturbed state of mind", leading to her taking her own life.

"It was only a rumour," the priest explained. "She reported that her assailant was a powerful man, a stranger who attacked her on her way home one afternoon.

"She would have been terrified about reporting it to her parents, let alone the village policeman," the old man said. "By the time she told her parents that she was pregnant, it was far too late to investigate. There were still Canadian and American servicemen moving through the district, so it could be true, but there was no way to find out. Your grandparents preferred to think it was an elaborate lie. Because there was a fair amount of gossip, needless to say. Those were hard times for unmarried mothers! And the war was confusing for everyone."

"Well, thank you, Father. Whatever the truth of it, it is a very sad story. I was born later in Oakmere. I haven't the least memory of my mother. I was brought up by her sister, Betty. I'm not sure how she regarded her younger sister. I do know that just three years after she had been taken in by her sister, my mother was in such a bad state that she ended her home life."

Father Kerswell looked at Frank with compassion. He knew about the suicide, he said.

He did not know more than the events as reported in the local press. It had happened when he was in the middle of his training at the seminary. He remembered the occasional comment from local residents. They were shocked and often embarrassed. Suicide was a sin, after all, but they were also aware of the consequences Madeleine's death had brought with it, an orphaned son and a sister and brother-in-law saddled with his care. There was some sadness that a young life had ended, and a great deal of curiosity as to the full reason. For the villagers, however, the most notable result had been that the Whitakers from that moment onwards kept themselves to themselves. But the war was coming to an end and everyone had other things to think about. The death of one young girl was not especially memorable among do many others.

Frank had plenty to think about on the short bus trip back to the town. What he had unearthed so far was a painful story. His earliest years had been especially unhappy, but he had been only dimly aware. He could not entirely understand or imagine how all these events had affected his aunt. She had picked up the pieces so to speak. She must have been more shocked than most. Perhaps he could glimpse something of the reason for her coldness towards him. He had often wondered why she and his uncle had not adopted him formally. Perhaps it was that she could not accept him as an individual without constantly linking him in her mind with his mother's death. He had learned a great deal, but now more than ever he was desperate to dig deeper by talking to his aunt, if she were still alive and if Steve could track her down and if she would agree to speak to him. All these ifs looked like a formidable barrier. More than ever now he missed Louise.

Back in Oakmere, he did a little shopping, returned for a while to the hotel and wrote an email to Poppy, giving her the basic information, but steering clear of any emotional comment. He answered several emails, including one from his neighbours, reassuring him that all was well, and then he walked back to Orchard Street for a pleasant meal, made more pleasant by the proximity of the husband-and-wife team. Between cooking and serving they exchanged a few comments. He told them of his countryside rambles. Despite eating a solitary meal, therefore, he felt part of the human race. As he walked back to the hotel, where he ordered a whiskey and soda in the public bar, he tried to subdue his impatience at the thought that he must now wait for Steve to complete his investigations. He suddenly realised that it was already Tuesday. He decided to spend the next day on a truly long walk along part of the South Downs Way. If he left early, say at eight o'clock, he could be on the track itself by nine. He would walk all the way to Amberley where he would find a suitable pub for lunch before walking back, if he had the energy, or find a local bus service back to his car. That would fill the day very well. Thursday, he remembered, was the evening of the Men's Shed Group. Yes, he would find things to do for a few days in this pleasant but sleepy little town.

The exercise did him a great deal of good. He was generally fit and used to a great deal of time spent out of doors. He knew in theory that exercise was good for the mind as well as the body and his long walk, which occupied most of Wednesday, proved the fact. When he woke on

Thursday morning, he congratulated himself because it was raining steadily. He had chosen the right day for his long walk. He was not sure how he would fill the day indoors. He was not a great reader, but he had brought with him a detective novel to pass the time. Jeremy served him a cooked breakfast. It was palatable but not especially appetising. Then he settled himself in the comfortable shabbiness of the lounge. He opened his laptop and found a message from Poppy.

Hi, Daddy, landed at Heathrow late last night. I now have a few days off! Can we meet? Give me a call when you get this. I hate being away from you at the moment and I'd like to make sure you're okay. Poppy XXX

Frank lost no time. Poppy was obviously worried about him. She said as much. For his part, Frank was eager to see her again. She had not been away all that long, but she was his one remaining link with Louise and she always brought joy with her. They discussed practicalities. She could catch a train as far as Guildford, she said. Was there room at the inn? While she waited, Frank asked Jeremy. Jeremy was quite startled but pleased at the thought of letting another room.

Poppy would catch an early train to Guildford the following morning, she said, having sorted out one or two things at her flat. Frank would drive up to Guildford and meet her in the station buffet sometime after 11 o'clock. He was excited at the prospect. He found it extremely difficult to settle after that. He borrowed an umbrella and walked down the road in the rain, excited like a child. Later he returned to the hotel and tried to read his book. His mind kept wandering. He could not stop himself trying to imagine the events surrounding his mother's banishment from her home in Larch. He had no details of how Betty had treated her, nor did he know anything about his own birth. There was still a mystery which came to a head with Madeleine's tragic decision to throw herself off the railway bridge. He had walked as far as the bridge and looked with horror down at the rails. The track was now disused.

He did his best to think of something else. He was surprised to find he was looking forward to the meeting of the Men's Shed Group that evening. They had made him remarkably welcome, accepting him without too many questions. He felt comfortable in their company.

They offered him, he realised, a remarkable degree of friendship. Although he was accustomed to spend most of his time at work on his own, having removed himself to this little town where he knew no one, he risked being isolated. It now struck him that the decision might not have been altogether wise. The loss of Louise had left him emotionally raw. He needed at the very least people that he knew around him, and he had chosen to leave them all behind. He had now spent several days in Oakmere and had been on his own for most of the time. He acknowledged to himself how much he appreciated the kindness of the one or two people he had met. As well as the Men's Shed Group, the couple that ran the Orchard Street restaurant, the old priest he had met in the village, Steve Blount, the solicitor, even Jeremy had all accepted him at face value. Nevertheless, the prospect of spending a day or two with his daughter lifted his spirits on this grey, rainy day.

The rain stopped early in the afternoon and he ventured out. He returned to the old shop in Orchard Street and bought an umbrella, pleasing the owner whose wrinkled face cracked into something approaching a smile. On one of the tables, he found a stack of CDs and DVDs. Idly, he looked through them and found a DVD of the film he had first seen with Louise many years before. He parted with 50p and took it away with him to his hotel room. He was able to watch it on his laptop. It was "Singing in the Rain." Normally, he would not have bothered, if it had not been for the memories it brought with it of sharing time with Louise. It was not a good copy – there were a few scratches which made the picture jump and interrupted the sound from time to time, but he watched it to the end. When he removed the disc from the machine, it was suddenly very quiet in his room. The music and the laughter had drained away. Outside his window the sky was a sullen grey and his mood plummeted. It was now late afternoon. Once more he left the Farmers Arms and returned to Orchard Street to the welcoming comfort of the restaurant. He treated himself to a good meal and a glass of red wine before returning to the inn.

It was difficult to believe that he had been here a week already, but Steve and the Doc arrived together and greeted him in the bar. When he joined them at their usual table, he was told politely not to occupy the visitors' chair because he was now a regular guest. The others drifted in, each collecting a glass of beer on their way. Frank had asked Jeremy to tell him what wines he had available before choosing one. The house wine, he thought, might be suspect, so he bought a bottle of decent claret. He would take what he did not drink or share back to his room later. He offered to share it with anyone who wanted a glass, but they all look mildly puzzled and shook their heads.

"We don't really trust the wine," said Pat. "At least we know what we're getting with the beer."

"Unlike you," said Gordon with a grim. "Bet you had a hell of a hangover."

"You can certainly say that," Frank admitted.

"Well, we are all glad you're still here," said Phil. "I don't mean we thought you might be dead. I'm surprised you find so much to do here. It's a pretty uninteresting place."

"I wouldn't say that," Frank replied. "Mind you, I did come here on a kind of mission."

"Ah! Not so much an alien, then, more missionary."

"Well, I suppose you have to admit," Gordon commented, "we are a generally heathen lot. Maybe we need to be saved or something. I don't remember ever having a missionary here before, even so."

"Stop pulling his leg," Steve said.

"No, not that kind of mission," said Frank. "I came here to try to trace some of my family connections."

"Any luck?"

Frank gave Steve a quick glance. He did not want to say too much. Steve remained impassive, giving no indication that he was privy to any information at all. His professional discretion was in full play.

"I managed to find the house where my grandparents used to live in Larch," Frank said.

"Oh! Not here then?"

"No, Larch. They are both dead, of course."

"Why of course? People live a very long time these days." It was Doc.

"Oh, granted," Frank agreed, "but I calculate they would now be somewhere between a hundred and ten and a hundred and twenty years old."

At this there was general laughter. The discussion moved on to other matters.

"We never asked," Phil said, when there was a pause in the general conversation," is your mission complete? Shall we see you again next week?"

"I can't be sure," Frank said. "I'm still tracking other members of the family."

"What about your wife?" It was Gordon, an innocent question, prompted possibly by the glint of gold on Frank's left hand.

"My wife died a month ago."

There was a shocked, respectful silence. Gordon apologised. There were embarrassed members around the table. This was something they had not been prepared for. No one knew what to say. It was Frank who broke the silence.

"You weren't to know," he said. "Part of the reason for coming here was to get away from – ," he did not know what it was he was running from. "I just needed to get away," he concluded lamely.

"I'm sorry," Gordon said again. "It really isn't any of our business."

"To be honest," Frank said, "I feel quite grateful to you all. Your Men's Shed Group is such a good idea. You've made me feel very welcome."

This merely caused more embarrassment.

"Anybody ready for a refill?" Steve asked.

"I'm happy to say," said Frank, as people shuffled around, emptied their glasses, or signalled to Steve that they needed a refill, "that my daughter is coming down tomorrow night to stay a couple of nights here."

"What, in the Farmers Arms?"

"Yes. It's actually quite comfortable. It's much shabbier than I remember, but the rooms are okay. You just have to remember not to drink the beer."

There was a murmuring laughter. They clearly appreciated the lightening of the mode.

"Where does your daughter live?" Phil asked.

"She works for an airline so she doesn't really spend a lot of time in any one place. She shares a flat in south London with two other air hostesses. They are coming and going all the time."

"Well!" Phil exclaimed. "That sounds very glamorous."

"I suppose it does," Frank agreed. "I don't think it would be for me, constantly on the move, shut up in a little cigar tube, looking after people who are busy getting drunk, never knowing from one week to the next where you are going to be, Hong Kong, Dubai, Sydney, Singapore..."

"If I were a bit younger," said Pat, "I'd go for it. A lot more exciting than this place."

Frank smiled. "I suppose so," he said," but even Poppy is beginning to get tired of it after just six years."?

"Poppy?"

"Yes. I suppose it is appropriate."

This comment provoked puzzled looks all round.

"I'm a professional gardener," Frank explained.

"A gardener? I don't think we've ever had a gardener in the Group."

Frank explained that he spent less and less time these days doing what he loved best, growing plants. He explained that he was in charge of the municipal gardens in his own town. It was a relatively novel topic for the Group and the rest of the evening was spent happily talking about their experiences growing things or of exotic gardens some had visited. It was just after eleven o'clock when Frank made his way back to his bedroom, clutching a bottle about one third full.

Chapter four

Poppy was at a small table opposite the door. She stood up as he entered the buffet, threw her arms around him, and gave him a long hug and a kiss.

"I'm sorry I'm a bit late," he said. It was eleven fifteen according to the large clock.

"You're not really late," she said. "We said between eleven and twelve."

"I would have been here half an hour ago," he said. "You won't believe this, but I was stopped and breathalysed."

"Breathalysed? Well, they obviously let you go, but why did they stop you in the first place? You are a pretty steady driver."

Frank grinned. "I was in too much of a hurry to see you," he said. "I'm afraid I was driving a couple of miles over the limit through the village. Just my luck that there was a police car parked there. They flagged me down and insisted on breathalysing me. I explained why I was in a hurry. They were actually very considerate but they pointed out that I was only a few points short of the limit. I didn't think about it. I drank rather more wine than usual last night."

"Daddy!" Poppy's tone was reproachful and concerned. "This is not like you!"

"No, I agree."

"Do you want a cup of coffee now you're here?"

"Not here. We can stop on the way back to Oakmere. I'm sure we can find somewhere on the road."

Poppy picked up her overnight bag with its smart, airline logo and they headed out of the station to the car park. Frank led the way towards the car, reaching in his pocket for the keys.

"Hand them over," Poppy commanded.

Frank was surprised but she was clearly serious. He handed her the keys with a smile and walked around to the passenger side. Poppy adjusted the seat and the driving mirrors, checked that he had done up his seatbelt, and drove competently to the exit.

"That was a bit of a shock," she said. "The last thing I expected were you to be in trouble with the law. You can see why I'm worried about you."

"Maybe this is the new, adventurous me," he said, grinning at her.

"Seriously though," she said, "how are you coping? Are you sleeping all right? Are you sure it was a good thing for you to set off on this trip? From what little you've told me so far it sounds as though you have only found out a lot of sad things. That's not what you need, surely. The last thing you want is more pain and suffering at the moment."

"It's a risk I knew I was running," Frank admitted. "After all these years I think I can accept whatever truth I turn up, however unpleasant it is. I don't expect you to fully understand how I feel about all this, but I'm not turning to drink, I promise."

"That's why I'm here," she said. "I understand how difficult it must be for you to discover that your mother took her own life, even if you can't remember her."

"There's no need for you to be affected by all this," he said. "I don't suppose it is of great interest to you to learn about my parentage, less still to learn about my grandparents."

"You're wrong," she said. "I want to know everything. My first concern is for you, but I can't help you if I don't understand what's going on and what you found out. So far it sounds very worrying to me."

"There's a large pub about a mile from here," Frank said. "It's on this side of the road."

"A pub? Surely you don't want to start drinking at this time of the day?"

Frank laughed. "It's a sort of roadhouse," he said. "I'm pretty sure it will serve coffee. Don't worry, I've told you I'm not turning to drink."

He was telling her about the Men's Shed Group when they pulled into the forecourt of the roadhouse. He explained how he had been invited to join them on the first night in the Farmers Arms and how he had joined them again. Poppy was reassured. It was good news that he had made friends in such a short time.

"I'm glad you found this group," she said as they found a table and took their drinks. "I was never sure it was a good idea to take yourself off into unknown territory, with no one to talk to."

"You forget I'm used to working on my own most of the time."

"Maybe so, but this is the time you need familiar faces round you."

Frank gazed fondly at his daughter as he considered what she said.

"Nobody can begin to take your mother's place," he said. "She would be the only person I could talk to."

"You could try me," Poppy said. She sounded hurt. "I know it's not the same, but I'm hurting too. And it would be good for me to share these things with you."

"I I'm so sorry," said Frank. "Of course, you are grieving too. I don't want to shut you out. You must know how important you are to me. I love you dearly."

Poppy looked him in the eye, her expression grave. All at once Frank saw a small child, one he had watched years ago, vulnerable, looking for a father to trust in. Neither of them spoke for a few minutes, their eyes alone exchanging unspoken messages.

"I want you to tell me all about your research," Poppy said at last. "It all sounds gloomy and depressing so far. I'm not sure it's good for you."

"It was certainly a shock to find my mother had taken her own life. I don't remember her at all." Frank acknowledged. "I still found I was quite affected by it. Strange!"

"Not really surprising. I suppose she would have been my granny. I was sad to hear the news, too. What drove her to it, do you know? She must have been dreadfully unhappy. After all, she was leaving a three-year-old behind."

Frank voiced the thoughts that hovered in both their minds. "She was very ill mentally," he said. "The balance of her mind was disturbed is what the coroner decided. It implies she was mad."

"Not a word we use these days," Poppy said. "Mentally ill. Whatever the facts are, at least it was not hereditary." She forced a grin, but they had both allowed the idea to pass through their minds.

"I don't know if you will understand," Frank said, "but I feel I need to know more. It all happened nearly sixty years ago. People have moved on, some have died. The records don't give the answers."

They returned to the car and resumed their journey to Oakmere. Jeremy treated the new guest like royalty. Frank was amused. He was proud of his daughter. She had achieved quite a lot in the course of her career to date, both at school and with the airline. But she was also a beautiful young woman who had inherited some of the most attractive features from her mother, including a glorious head of hair. He was not surprised at Jeremy's reaction. But Frank was also beginning to realise there was a lot he did not know about his daughter. She had always been closer to her mother. He could not even remember the name of her current boyfriend.

Poppy was accustomed to living out of her small suitcase. She settled into her room, which she said was perfectly comfortable and spotless, then rejoined Frank in the lounge. Jeremy hurried over to offer tea or coffee. They refused and walked out into the little town. Poppy had never been there before. They wandered round the streets, visited the church because it seemed the appropriate thing to do, and found their way back to Orchard Street where they ate a light meal. The conversation was almost entirely concerned with the shops and buildings. They were both for the moment content just to share time together. As they entered Orchard Street and headed for the restaurant, Frank was conscious for the first time that Poppy was holding his hand. The realisation was mildly confusing, a mixture of pride and remembering yet again holding that same hand when it was much smaller.

After the meal he led her across the road to the old shop. Poppy was amused by her father's apparent interest in a down at heel, second hand shop in a side street. Frank explained that his uncle had once owned the shop and it had been a pawnbrokers.

"A pawnbrokers!" This was something outside Poppy's experience. "Your uncle was a pawnbroker?"

"Yes, he was. I don't even know where he came from. He wasn't English. The name is very odd, Kristinin. It's another part of the mystery."

"You have never spoken of him to me," Poppy said. "What was he like?"

Frank took a few moments to think about his answer. "I didn't have very much to do with him really," he said at last. "Our paths crossed in the morning sometimes, but I was usually getting ready to go to school or finishing the chores which my aunt set for me. He spent all day in the shop, so he didn't get home until well after six o'clock. I was banished to my bedroom by about seven thirty in the evening."

"Did you eat together?"

"Do you know, we never did. I suppose that sounds extraordinary. It's one of the things that make me feel I was always on the outside, so to speak."

"What about weekends and holidays?"

"We never seem to go on holiday together. I don't remember much about weekends, either. Sundays always seemed dreary unless I was off exploring."

"It sounds like a very miserable childhood."

"It was all I knew." Frank frowned. "I enjoyed exploring the woods especially, but it was a solitary life for a boy, I suppose."

Poppy gave his hand a sympathetic squeeze. "But what did your uncle look like?" she asked. "Have you got any photographs?"

"Not one. I don't even have a picture of Aunt Betty. You'd think there would be pictures of the two of them somewhere, but I don't remember seeing one. Uncle Vlad was a small man, much older than Betty. I didn't think much about it at the time, but I'm not sure that they got on very well together."

"You know, you've never told me any of this before. It sounds like a truly miserable childhood."

"As I said, it was all I knew. I had no real means of comparing it. I just escaped whenever I could. That's why I became interested in the environment. I realise that nature probably is red in tooth and claw, but I could at least understand that. And a lot of it was very interesting and beautiful."

This, Poppy realised, signalled a new insight for her. She had always got on well with both her parents, although her father at times struck her as a little reserved, uncommunicative. Now she was beginning to understand him better. She was grateful. This time spent together was suddenly very precious.

Over the course of the next two days Frank explained everything that he had so far discovered. It was not much, he admitted, and a great deal depended on the enquiries that Steve Blount, the solicitor had agreed to undertake. He told Poppy about that. She was beginning to understand how important this was for him, but she also remained concerned about what he might discover. It was still possible that Madeleine had suffered from some form of mental weakness which might be passed on. That seemed unlikely but lack of knowledge left room for the imagination. Or was there some other, possibly sinister reason for Madeleine's suicide? Whatever the truth, it might well be the reason that Betty had kept silent all these years. Indeed, the entire family seemed dysfunctional: Madeleine's parents had thrown her out and completely denied her story that she had been raped, preferring to blame her and accuse her of what they saw as grossly immoral or sinful behaviour. She had at least hung on to her son, though it had only been for three years. That could not have been easy. She would have been viewed as "a fallen woman" and burdened by shame. So, if she had fought so strongly to keep her illegitimate son, how had she managed to leave him as an orphan in the care of her sister? She had lived with Betty and her husband for three years. What kind of relationship had there been in that unhappy household?

Together, Poppy and her father took the trip back out to the village of Larch. This time they met no one to talk to. Frank told her about the conversation with the old priest. He then led the way to the cottage where Madeleine's parents had lived and where she had been born. After searching a little, they found a path at the back of the cottage and a footpath across the fields that led to the wood. This, they agreed, must have been the path which Madeleine had used daily to return from her job as a maid in the "big house," the old Manor, the other side of the trees. It had now been converted into flats. Frank was interested in the pathway, however. It was very seldom used nowadays and was overgrown in places on the fringe of the wood, but it was still visible under the trees, a track which wound for maybe two hundred yards. Madeleine could well have been attacked here, as she had repeatedly claimed was the case. She had not reported the attack at the time, which is why her father had refused to accept it as true. It seemed he preferred to believe his young daughter was, in his own words, "a dirty slut." Frank found it very hard to come to terms with such behaviour on the part of his own grandfather. Poppy found it almost impossible to believe. Had Betty believed the story her sister told? Whether she had believed it or no, she had at least taken her in. Her reputation would doubtless have been affected as the elder sister.

They made their way back to the main street of Larch. At a small, shop they bought ice creams and sat on a wall together to wait for the bus back to Oakmere. It was a pleasant, slightly overcast day. They had only fifteen minutes to wait for the bus and their heads were so full of thoughts, speculation, emotions, questions that they did not speak. They were content to sit, cheek by jowl and wait.

"What next?" Poppy asked. They were back in the Farmers Arms, drinking tea, served by the admiring Jeremy.

"I just have to wait and hope that Steve Blount makes contact with Aunt Betty."

"And if not?"

"If not, the trail will be at an end," said Frank. "Perhaps we are destined never to know the full story."

"I'm not altogether sure in your place I would want to know the whole story," said Poppy.

"Having got this far, I just have to go on. The whole thing is tragic, but I just need to know the truth, whatever that is. I can't go to my grave never knowing."

Poppy threw him a startled look. "Go to your grave?" she said in alarm. "Daddy, you've got decades in front of you yet. Don't talk like that, please!"

"Sorry," he said, "it was only a figure of speech, and not the way it was meant to sound."

"Thank God for that! It's time we did something to cheer ourselves up," Poppy said. "I know you're here to pursue this strange quest of yours, but it is really very depressing, you know. We need to think of something other than death and suicide and the misery and pain of all those years ago. There isn't much we can do about it. The past is the past. We have to be able to put it behind us, let it go."

"I know. I also realise that it's all harder for me than for you. This is my past, not yours."

"Madeleine would have been my granny," Poppy repeated, "and we are talking about your early childhood, yours, my father's. But you are right, I think I could walk away from the mystery, if I had to. I had a lovely childhood, thanks to you and Mummy. I miss her like hell."

This simple statement brought them both to tears for a moment.

"Come on!" Poppy dried her eyes, and stood up briskly. "Where's your car?"

"Outside, in the car park."

"Give me the keys," she said. He smiled at her tone of command and handed them over.

"Where are we going?" he asked.

"A mystery tour."

She drove along quiet, country roads. On either side cattle grazed in the fields. The hedgerows were lush and green. With the windows down, the fresh air blew her hair into a halo.

"Do you realise," she asked, "this is one of the best counties in terms of trees? There is more woodland here than almost anywhere else in England."

"I sort of knew that," he said in a deliberately dry tone.

She laughed, realising that she was talking to a professional horticulturalist. It was good to hear her laugh and her high spirits were infectious. As they climbed the crest of a rise and swooped down the other side, Frank felt happier than he had at any time since the funeral. He was suddenly grateful for Poppy's cheerfulness and vigour. He reached across and kissed her on the cheek, surprising her. However, she said nothing, merely smiled at him and continued driving until they reached the outskirts of a seaside town. She found a parking space on the prom and led Frank down to the sand. She got him to roll up his trousers and, barefoot, they ran and splashed in the shallow water. Frank found himself laughing. This simple, almost childish pleasure, running hand in hand, had turned his dark and burdened mood into carefree exuberance. It did not last long, but it was enough to make him understand that life still held happiness.

Afterwards, they wondered along the seafront, past all the tourist shops with their plastic buckets, inflatable ducks, some hats, flimsy shrimp nets and racks of picture postcards. They ate ice creams and, a little later, they sat in a cheap café and ate fish and chips. With sand in his shoes, Frank was remembering the days when Poppy was a small child, holding a parent by each hand, laughing, and swinging her feet along other, similar promenades, exploring rock pools, driving home, contented, and tired, Poppy asleep in the back of the car. He had so much to be thankful for. Most of all, he was thinking, he had a lovely daughter.

He insisted on driving back to Oakmere. Poppy, he said, had done her share and he hadn't touched alcohol all day. They were both weary, too tired to think any further about the reasons for being so far from home. Neither spoke of the one thing that was uppermost in their minds. Poppy was due back on duty the following evening. Back in the Farmers Arms, they drank tea in Frank's room before she kissed him good night and went to bed. Frank smiled at the sight of the sand washed off in the shower, then he got into bed, images of the day whirling in his head. As usual, he was very conscious of the empty space beside him. He had deliberately left the curtains drawn and could see the moon peeping out from the clouds which drifted across. It would take him a long time to get to sleep, he thought, but his head was full of pleasant memories and he fell asleep quickly.

Chapter five

Frank left the station where he had seen Poppy onto her train. It was still only mid-morning. His stomach reminded him that he was hungry and he found somewhere for a late breakfast. Poppy's departure left him feeling lonelier than he had ever felt in his life. He was trying to grow used to the ache in his heart which Louise's death had left, but the short time he had spent with his daughter had been wonderful. She had her own life to return to, something he was always conscious of, but now he was overtaken by a sense of desolation. He ate the meal hurriedly and without enjoyment, then he made his way back to the car park to begin the journey back to Oakmere. He was so lonely he felt almost ill. He drove slowly, one eye on the speedometer. He had no wish to be stopped again by the police. He was back at the Farmers Arms soon after midday. He left his car in the car park and walked as far as the bench overlooking the river. There he sat, unaware of the time, as waves of self-pity washed over him. He wept. His emotions were a total jumble of self-pity, of genuine grief and of vivid, happy memories of years gone by as well as of the time he had spent with Poppy. Their relationship had somehow changed. The love he felt for her as a daughter now merged into an intimate friendship with an adult. Perhaps part of his grief, he thought, might be at the loss of his little girl, who had somehow changed into this adult he had grown to know. He sat in this quiet wood for hours until the beauty and tranquillity awakened him. The river still splashed and swirled. The birds still sang. A light breeze fluttered the leaves above his head. He stood up, blew his nose vigorously, squared his shoulders and walked determinedly back into town.

He went back to the hotel. Someone had tidied his room, but had not touched his personal belongings. His laptop sat on the bedside table. He opened it and found three messages from friends and acquaintances, asking how he was, wishing him well. He did not know how to reply. He typed something meaningless and closed the lid. It was very quiet in this room. He realised he had just about exhausted the potential of Oakmere. It was a pleasant little town but most of the memories that came with it were sad ones, especially the railway bridge which he now knew was where his mother had died. Barrett Street had not aroused strong feelings. He had no wish to reconnect with the old Grammar School. His only reason for being there any longer was to wait for news from Steve Blount. But even if Steve was able to track down Aunt Betty, he could just as easily send the information by email or even telephone him. There was no real reason for him to stay any longer. The Men's Shed would reassemble the following evening. He would stay long enough for that. He was grateful to these men for their kindness in making him welcome, so he would spend one more evening in their company and leave the following morning. He would probably find it better to be back at home. Part of the reason for leaving had been the prospect of having to live on his own in a house where every room, every object, from the door handles to the soft furnishings spoke of Louise. He had been running away, although his search for the details of his mother's death was a genuine reason. He went down to Reception and explained he would be leaving on the Friday morning.

He spent much of the intervening time making a written record of what he had so far discovered. It was not great literature, but it helps clarify what he knew by writing it down chronologically. It also made the gaps in his knowledge more obvious. Where such gaps emerged, he wrote the questions he needed to find answers to.

What, if anything, was the trigger which had driven Madeleine to take her own life?

Was her crisis sudden, or the result of months or years of mental ill health?

Why had his uncle and aunt never formally adopted him?

What had been the relationship between Madeleine and her sister?

Had he imagined the poor relationship between his aunt and his uncle?

Had anyone ever investigated Madeleine's claim that she had been raped?

Was there any way in which he could identify his biological father?

Until or unless Steve Blount managed to track Aunt Betty, assuming she was willing to answer some of the questions, he would never get the answers. He had done all he could here. He spent his last day in Oakmere revisiting the places he had grown to like. He also paid one last visit to the second-hand shop, bought the latest edition of the local paper, ate a pleasant meal in Orchard Street, then packed his bags ready for an early departure the following day before joining the Men's Shed Group.

As usual, they made him welcome. They did not ask him personal questions, other than to comment on his daughter. Two or three of them had seen him with her. They were interested in her job as a flight attendant and the conversation wandered as it always seemed to do. Frank was particularly careful not to drink very much. They expressed surprise when he stopped after one pint of beer. When he explained that he had been close to the limit the previous week, they laughed but they understood his caution. Afterwards, he could not say that he had enjoyed the evening. "Enjoyed" would be too strong a word. The acceptance by these men afforded an unexpected degree of comfort and he was grateful for that. He left them still chatting a little while before Jeremy called last orders. He explained he wanted to get away early in the morning. He had given his email address and telephone number to Steve Blount, who took it without comment. There was a chorus of goodbyes and Frank made his way back to his room. He lay awake for several hours.

The following morning, he settled the bill, gave Jeremy a welcome tip, and was on his way by 8 o'clock. The journey was uneventful and as he turned into his driveway Jack appeared from next door.

"Home again," his neighbour greeted him. "Are you back for good, or is this a quick visit?"

"It's permanent," Frank said. He thanked Jack for looking after the property. The two men chatted for a few minutes. Frank said little about his trip to Oakmere. It was, he said, the place where he had spent his childhood. Of course, he said, it had changed after such a long time, but it had been interesting to go back.

"Do you have any family there?" Jack asked.

"Not now."

Jack left him to unload his things and Frank went into the empty house. He opened all the ground floor windows before he made himself a pot of tea. He had bought a few basic supplies but he would have to make a visit to the supermarket in the morning. He sat in the kitchen where Jack had left a pile of letters and advertising circulars. He put the circulars in the recycling box and looked through the letters. One envelope contained a card which he expected would be a belated sympathy card. He glanced at it and was pleasantly surprised to find it was a notelet with a cheerful picture. It was from Janice Chessington, Deputy Head of St Agnes School, and one of Louise's closest friends.

Dear Frank

At a meeting of the PTA ten days ago there was general agreement that we should find some way of creating a memorial for Louise. As several people put it, she had done a huge amount for the school, and for the children and parents. It won't be long before we shall be receiving the children of some of those children! The following day we floated the suggestion in a letter to all the parents, past and present, who had known Louise. The result was quite astonishing.

If everybody who responded honours the pledges they have given, we should have a substantial amount of money. The members of the PTA felt that the most appropriate memorial might be a tree to be planted in the area near the very successful garden which, she told me once, you helped her set up. As I'm sure you know, it has provided great pleasure to generations of small children who have learned the rudiments of gardening and have been introduced to the wonders of nature.

You are the obvious person to advise on the type of tree we should purchase. Could you please contact me to discuss the idea? If you agree to this, we shall arrange a special ceremony and, if you agree, you will be asked to plant the new addition. I do hope you agree. Please give me a ring when you feel able to.

Much love from Janice.

Frank picked up the phone and called Janice's number. He had a picture of her in his mind's eye, warm, motherly, always busy, always smiling. He wondered if she was going to take over as Head Teacher. She would probably do an excellent job. Like Louise, she was well liked by the children. She had chaired the PTA for as long as he could remember. When she answered his call, her first enquiry was about his health and how was he coping. He was doing all right, he said, and thanked her for the note.

"If you are at home," she said, "perhaps I could come and talk about this with you. I understand that you have been away. In fact, I am surprised you are at home now. I don't suppose you feel like socialising much, and I can only imagine how much you are missing Louise. I think of her myself every day."

"You will always be welcome, Janice. I'm not sure that I can think straight as yet, but it would be nice to see you anyway."

They arrange for her to call on him in the evening. "I have nothing much else to do," he said. He rang off, sorted the rest of the correspondence, then made a quick trip to the supermarket and came home with a quantity of food and drink. It took him some time to put it all away. He heated up a ready meal, turned it out on a plate and ate in the kitchen. As soon as he stopped moving, he began to feel the same bleak emptiness. Out of habit he washed up and threw the plastic tray into the recycling box.

From the garden came the sound of birdsong. Inside, the big house was silent. When he and Louise had bought the property thirty years previously with the help of Louise's parents, they recognised just how big the old farmhouse was. They did not really need five bedrooms, nor two sitting rooms. The property was cheap, however, and the huge piece of land would make a wonderful garden. There had also been some half-serious suggestions about needing lots of rooms for the hoped-for family. The discussion had been because they had wanted at least four children. That dream was not to be realised. Now that Poppy had long ago left, and Louise no longer would use one bedroom as a workshop and another as an office, Frank felt like a tiny snail with an enormous shell on its back. The silence made matters worse. He turned on music in one of the sitting rooms at full volume and left all the doors open. The main effect was to drive the sleepy cat out into the garden. Frank turned off the music after a while. The house was far too big, but the garden was another matter. He and Louise had poured effort and love into it. Frank could not think of losing his precious garden.

Janice arrived. She put her arms around him and gave him a kiss and said yes, she'd love a cup of tea which she watched him make. He carried it through to the sitting room and put it down on a small table.

"The appeal, or rather the response, has been incredible," she said. "Louise was loved by everyone. We suggested they might like to pledge five or ten pounds, but many of them have given much, much more. We had suggested that we could plant a tree in her memory. You and Louise started the garden all those years ago and it is still a popular part of the school life. A tree seemed like a very good memorial. You are the obvious person to advise us."

"It's a lovely idea," Frank said. "You can buy a decent tree for about a hundred pounds. It won't be very big, of course, but it will grow."

Janice was smiling at him. "I think we can do better than that," she said. "How about four hundred and fifty?"

Frank gaped. He was not expecting such generosity. "You could buy a mature tree for that," he said. "You might even have money left over to buy things like extra tools or even seeds or what about new cold frames? The old ones are beginning to look a little tired, if I remember."

"That's not all," said Janeice delighted to have surprised him, "Jeff Peterson's three children were all pupils in St Agnes."

Jeff Peterson was well known to Frank. He ran the Garden Centre.

"Mr Peterson pointed out that he only stocks small trees."

"Well," said Frank, "little trees grow into big ones of course, but if you're committee is really keen to buy a mature tree, in my job I have dealings with a grower. I imagine you don't want to offend Mr Peterson, though."

"I don't think he would be offended, because he said he was quite happy to donate garden furniture instead. He suggested a bench."

This conversation about gardening and landscaping was at the same time interesting and comfortable for Frank, who had spent years dealing with such things in his professional capacity. He agreed willingly to meet the other members of this group to discuss what they had in mind and make appropriate suggestions for a memorial tree. Planting a mature tree would demand careful planning and the use of a front-end loader as well as a small, mechanical digger to make a large hole. When Janice left, Frank phoned his deputy at work. Bill was surprised to hear from him. They discussed suitable trees, given the location and the soil, agreed on the slow-release fertiliser and compost as well as the machinery they would need.

"Sounds like you're missing the job," Bill commented. "Have you changed your mind? You thinking of coming back again early after all?"

"No, apart from this job. It's rather special, as I expect you understand."

"Me and the boys will be honoured to be part of it," he said.

Frank switched off his phone. Bill's remark about going back to his job made him think. All the time he had been talking to both Bill and Janice he had felt fully engaged, his grief temporarily forgotten. However, he did not really want to go back to work yet. It was obvious to him that he needed to keep himself as busy as possible. His own garden was in good shape. He and Louise had enjoyed working on it together. The house itself, though comfortable and tidy, was not only full of reminders of Louise, it was also full of small defects which he had meant to deal with for a long time. There was a creaking floorboard which he trod on every morning, for one thing, and Louise's "office," a bedroom in which she kept everything to do with her work, as well as her workroom, was now redundant. He would have to sort out the piles of papers and books, the sewing stuff. He knew he would also have to deal with Louise's clothes, but he would wait until Poppy could help with that task. He knew it would be very upsetting. The study was another matter. He would clear it of clutter and redecorate.

Once he began to think about reorganising the house, he also began slowly to wonder if he should think of moving. The house was obviously too big for him. His Council Tax bill was ridiculous. He loved the garden and he did not really want to move away from the present community. The more he thought about it the less certain he was. If he were to stay here, in fact, whether he were to move or not at some point in the future, he could really do with some domestic help. It was unfortunate that Mrs Barnes, who had helped for an hour a day, had moved away just three weeks earlier. He was capable of using a Hoover and at a pinch he could stuff dirty washing into the washing machine and even hang it on the washing line, but he did not like the prospect of ironing. He was certainly able to cook for himself – he would prefer to do so. He had no idea what kind of wage a cleaner would expect. These were practical considerations he had not even thought of until now. He would ask friends and neighbours for advice about the domestic help. He would discuss the future of the house itself with Poppy in the first instance. He knew she was growing tired of her work. She might want to come home. He did not want to intrude upon her life, and living in the same house might not be what she wanted. Widowhood, he concluded, was a strange and complicated condition for which he had been ill-prepared.

His concerns about employing a cleaner were pre-empted by a call from Janice. She hoped he would not be offended, but it had occurred to her that he might appreciate some domestic help. One of her parents, a young, single mother with two children under the age of eight, had told her that she was looking for domestic work. Children, she pointed out, were expensive. Her problem was that she needed a job during school hours because she had to deliver and collect her children at school. She was a nice woman, according to Janice, but it was up to Frank. He thought about the idea for a while before
ringing her back and asking her to put this young woman, Kylie James, in touch so that he could arrange an interview.

Kylie turned up on time and Frank talked to her in the kitchen diner. She was a little shy but seemed ready to take on cleaning and the laundry two mornings a week. Hesitantly, she explained that there might be a problem during the school holidays, when she would need to be looking after her two children, Oliver, 8, and Emma, 6. Their father, she explained, had "gone off with a younger model and would not be back." Frank accepted the information without comment. He was secretly and ashamedly relieved; he knew it was prejudice on his part, but the phrase "unmarried mother" left him feeling uncomfortable.

"Could the children not come with you?" Frank asked.

"Are you sure?"

"Well, it will be fine, provided they are not going to use the beds as trampolines or have fights squirting tomato juice at one another. And it's a big garden."

Kylie laughed. "No, they are not badly behaved," she said. "Are you sure that's okay? It's very accommodating of you."

"If the worst comes to the worst," Frank replied with a straight face, "I can always go out for the morning."

Kylie stared at him, not sure whether to take him seriously or not. They discussed hours and wages and she agreed to make a start the following morning. He liked the girl, who was respectful and seemed intelligent. She had known Louise and, a little awkwardly expressed her condolences. When he was left on his own again, Frank hoped he would not regret the decision to allow a comparative stranger into his house. She would necessarily be touching and handling belongings which had been those of his wife. He was not entirely comfortable with the prospect of having a woman wandering through all the rooms, but he told himself firmly this was one of those changes he had to accept.

He took Bill with him to the Arboretum to look at trees. He was glad of the company and of the advice. It was good to share the day with Bill. The house felt more empty than usual when he got home. He could easily send a picture of the proposed tree by email, but instead he chose to phone Janice and talk to her in person. Her husband opened the door. Frank knew him only slightly. He explained the purpose of his visit as Janice appeared behind her husband. They both asked him in. They asked him to stay for a meal and he accepted, feeling reluctant to go back to his empty house until he had to. He showed them the pictures not only of the tree he had reserved, but also pictures of the rest of the Arboretum. They were both impressed and thought they might drive out there themselves just to look at the trees, some in flower. They were good hosts, listening to Frank expound on a subject which he knew well. He had first fallen in love with trees as a boy all those years ago in Oakmere.

The friendship and companionship were good for him. Perhaps Bill was right and he should think about going back to work after all. He decided not to make such a decision for a while.

The "Louise Memorial Committee" approved wholeheartedly of the recommended tree and sent a deposit to the Arboretum while they discussed the complicated arrangements they had in mind. Frank was not closely involved with these, though they asked him when he would be available for the tree planting ceremony. He said he had no intention of going anywhere for the immediate future. It was Bill who was responsible for the complicated arrangements. The mature tree, with a very large and extremely heavy root ball would be delivered by the Arboretum to the school. At that point Bill was in charge. He arranged for a mini-excavator to dig a very large hole. A front-end loader would move the tree to its final place which had been prepared with appropriate fertiliser and so on. The PTA wanted the process to be watched by the children, so Bill arranged for that part of the school grounds to be roped off. A Janice asked Frank to come along. She would like him to have a photograph taken next to the tree, she said. He agreed in order to humour her. The planting would take place, she said, on a Saturday morning. It would probably mean paying overtime to the men from the Parks and Gardens Department, but Frank shrugged. That would be up to Bill to sort out. For two weeks he heard nothing more, then he receives a note from Janice, with the date and time, 11 AM, and a reminder that he would be asked to have his photograph taken.

Chapter six

The day before the tree planting ceremony, Poppy arrived. He was delighted to see her. To celebrate the occasion, he took her out to dinner. At a nearby table, a party of six had ordered a meal. They looked at Frank and Poppy and seemed unusually interested. Frank looked at his daughter and thought they must have the wrong idea. They must be thinking he was too old to be entertaining such a glamorous young girl. He smiled, causing Poppy to look at him in puzzlement.

"I take it you can come with me to see the tree being planted?" He asked.

"Oh yes, I wouldn't miss it for anything. They must think a lot of Mummy to do this for her."

Frank agreed. He was still touched by the scale of the donations received.

George and Ann drove down for the ceremony Poppy insisted on driving Frank to the school. It was close on 10:30 as she drove through the gates. She gasped. Parents had walked there with their children as usual, but there were at least a dozen cars. One of them was from the local radio station. Janice and her husband stepped forward to greet the four of them. They led the way to the garden which Frank and Louise had started so many years before. From a rear entrance Bill's team of eight men, all of whom Frank knew well, was clustered near a front-end loader. In the large bucket sat the root ball of the tree. The branches had been tied carefully to protect them in transit. Lying down it looked enormous. A large, empty hole was waiting on the other side of a colourful ribbon. Chairs were arranged on either side of the green area surrounding the garden itself. Behind the tables tablecloths hinted at food and drink. Just beyond the ribbon to right and left were large speakers and a microphone on a stand stored in the middle. This was far more than Frank had been prepared for. Poppy gripped his arm and gave it a squeeze has Janice led them to chairs at the front and on the right. On either side, as they moved towards the front, friendly faces smiled and heads nodded in recognition.

"What on earth have you planned?" Frank asked.

"This is for Louise," said Janice firmly. "Don't you dare say anything against it."

Poppy's eyes were brimming with tears. Ann was also emotional. George looked a little dazed. Frank, embarrassed and overwhelmed, turned his attention to where Bill and his workmen stood, looking slightly anxious. Partly screened by the tractor and by bushes, a furniture van was parked. As he looked, he sensed movement behind him and he turned in time to see the mayor take his seat opposite where he sat with his daughter.

It was eleven o'clock. Janice left his side and stepped up to the microphone. She welcomed the mayor, the parents and children on behalf of the PTA.

"Louise Whitaker was a well-loved head teacher," she said, "just how loved and respected was made apparent when the Parent Teachers Association invited past pupils and parents to commemorate her passing by funding a small memorial. We were all astonished and moved by the response. Some of you will remember that when she was an assistant teacher at St Agnes, she and her husband, Frank started this garden. It is an established part of the school and the children enjoy working on it. It seemed only appropriate, therefore, to plant a tree in Louise's memory. Frank Whitaker and the Parks and Gardens Department have helped us choose the lovely tree which about to be planted."

There was applause at this, but Janice held up a hand.

"One of the parents here today is Mr Jeff Peterson. Mr Peterson wanted to make a special contribution of his own. Once the tree is well and truly planted, he will set up a special bench."

There was more applause.

"Here we go!" said Janice.

Slowly the tractor moved forward, the men watching carefully to steady it on either side. The great shovel was lowered and the gardeners steadied the large tree. Four of them held it upright while the other used shovels to fill the hole. They trod it in, watched by parents, children, and guests. Once Bill was satisfied with the installation, he picked up a pair of long-handled shears and, starting at the top, he cut the tapes which held the branches in place. The onlookers were entranced as the branches were freed. Poppy, unlike the others, was watching her father's face. She was worried. He was experiencing intense emotion and he was crying. She took a tissue from her handbag and handed it to him unobtrusively. Frank was remembering a time many years in the past. Louise had long hair which she wore in a coil high on her head for convenience during the day. Every evening she unpinned it and allowed it to cascade over her shoulders until one day she had it cut short. Frank hated it at first. They had fought and there had been tears. Frank grew to like the new style in time. The sight of the branches, as the tapes were cut, tumbling. He did not explain. With an occasional touch from helping hands, the tree was revealed in all its splendour. There were cries of appreciation and more applause and Bill and his helpers moved the tractor out of the way.

From behind the bushes the furniture van backed into view. The rear doors were opened and two men brought out a curved, wooden bench. It was followed by three more. The audience watched as the four sections were arranged to form a circle round the new tree and bolted together.

Janice had seized Frank's arm. He did not understand what she intended before she was standing with him in front of the microphone.

"I hope you agree," the microphone boomed," Louise would be pleased." She pushed the microphone towards him.

"She – she would be – "Frank was choked with emotion. "She. – overwhelmed," he stammered, wishing he could be buried with the new tree. But Poppy had swiftly come to his side. She kissed him, then, her own voice a little tremulous, she spoke into the microphone. "Thank you, thank you on behalf of the Whitaker family, including my grandmother and grandfather" She pointed to Ann and George.

There was no need to say more. Everyone was applauding again. Poppy helped her father escape to behind the ribbons where they both thanked Bill and his gang, then thanked Jeff Peterson.

"She deserved it," said Jeff, before climbing into the cab of the lorry to return to his garden centre.

For a few minutes Frank returned to his chair to stare at the tree and the encircling bench. It was a superb memorial.

Janice made her way through the throng of guests who were now busy trying to carry on casual conversations, while balancing cups of tea and paper plated loaded with sandwiches and pastries.

"Frank," she said, "I'm sorry if I embarrassed you. We couldn't let the cat out of the bag too early."

"I must have looked such a fool!" he said.

"No, you didn't. You just looked completely overwhelmed. And, as I keep saying, this wasn't your day, it was Louise's."

George and Ann left soon after the ceremony to drive home. Frank was very glad Poppy was there to drive him home later. She could see how deeply he had been moved by the ceremony. She made no attempt to engage in conversation. Frank was in a state of shock. He sat in his favourite chair for a long time and at last he fell asleep. She draped a rug round him then watched television with the sound turned down.

Chapter seven

The next day, Sunday, felt like an anticlimax. It was very quiet. Poppy took a mug of coffee out into the large garden and was standing on the paved terrace, listening to the sound of church bells, when Frank came to join her.

"How are you feeling?" she asked.

"Still a bit dazed," he said, putting an arm round her shoulders.

"They did Mummy proud, didn't they?"

He agreed. "I wondered if it wasn't, well, a bit over the top."

Poppy laughed. "It was great," she said.

"Your mother loved this place."

It was so obvious it needed no answer.

"I don't mean the town; I'm thinking of this house and garden."

"It's home," said Poppy.

"It wasn't like this when we moved in," Frank said. "We made it like this over the years. I could probably tell you the dates when we planted every tree and shrub. I certainly remember buying the new lawnmower. I almost fell off the ladder when I repaired the guttering." He smiled and looked up at the roof. They stood for a while in companionable peace. The bells had fallen silent. Birds twittered and sang in the trees which Frank and Louise had planted and which now produced an abundance of fruit.

"The truth is," Frank said, turning to face the house, "it's too big for me on my own. I don't need five bedrooms. I don't even need a separate sitting room, let alone two of them; the kitchen-diner is enough. It was your mother's favourite room. What would you say if I said I should put the property on the market?"

"What? Tell me you are joking! You can't sell this!" It was Poppy's turn to be shocked and alarmed.

"It's far too big for one man," Frank repeated.

"Please think about it. You and Mummy worked so hard to get the place how you wanted. It's full of memories for me, too. You can't sell it. At the very least don't do anything yet, not until – until -."

"Until I've got over losing your mother? That will never happen. I know I will learn to live with the situation in time, though I don't know how as yet. I miss her every day. And apart from the property being too big for me every room, every blade of grass reminds me of her." Poppy held him in her arms and they both cried. After a while Poppy let go of him.

"I've spilled coffee all down your pullover," she said. "Come on back to the kitchen. I'll make some fresh coffee while you find a clean top, then we can sit down and talk about this sensibly."

"OK," Frank said, following her through the patio doors." I can't think of any alternatives. Selling up is the only rational decision, even if it's in the future."

It was Poppy's turn to be worried. Father and daughter sat in the kitchen-diner and talked for a long time. Alternative courses of action ranged from unlikely and undesirable to fantastic. They included simply renting out the property, turning it into a bed and breakfast business, arranging for it to become a (temporary) home for refugees, dividing the house to make a smaller flat for Frank and a second flat to be let.

"Do you realise," Frank remarked at last, "it's three o'clock and we haven't thought about lunch. It's too late for a pub lunch. Looks like bread and cheese."

Poppy had other ideas. She took her father out to the car and drove out of town. It was a matter of ten miles to a location Frank had not visited for years, an artificial lake. Poppy parked the car outside the wooden building. On the side overlooking the water there was a small café where they ate a modest lunch of salad. Afterwards they hired a boat for an hour and explored the lake, learning in turns how to use the oars. When they climbed into the car to drive home, Frank thanked Poppy. He had enjoyed himself. He had even laughed as they had shared the time. Neither of them put it into words, but they were freshly aware that life could still be pleasurable.

Poppy was due back at Heathrow on Wednesday. She met Kylie and liked her. On Tuesday morning she and Frank sat either side of the breakfast table and checked their emails. Frank exclaimed in surprise. Poppy looked up.

"A message from Steve Blount," Frank explained. "He's the solicitor in Oakmere. He has found Aunt Betty."

"Aunt Betty?"

"I told you about her, the aunt who brought me up."

"Oh, does that make her my great-aunt?"

"Yes. The point is, I had completely lost touch with her."

"Didn't you say she was not very kind to you when you lived with her?"

"Yes, I was glad to get away from her."

"So, why are you looking for her now?"

"She's the only person who can tell me about my mother, your grandmother. I told you she killed herself when I was three."

"Are you sure you want to find out more?" Poppy peered at him over her computer screen. "Don't you think it might be painful? "

"I know you want to protect me," said Frank, "but this is something I have to do."

"Does this man say where your Aunt Betty is now? How old is she, anyway?"

"She's still alive. Steve asks me to phone him. That sounds hopeful."

Poppy closed her laptop to see him better. "I'm really worried about this," she said. "If your friend wants to arrange for you to meet Aunt Betty, I'd like to come with you. Would you mind?"

He smiled at her. "I'd love you to come with me, if we can arrange it, but what about your work?"

"Well, I haven't told you as yet, but it will all be much easier as from next month."

He said nothing, merely looked at her quizzically.

"I'm changing to ground crew. I shall be training flight attendants. No more flying – well, only short trips of an hour or so. It means more regular hours. Oh, and more pay. It means I'll get more time to be with Martin."

"Congratulations!" Frank hardly knew her boyfriend. He liked him, but Poppy had never shared any confidences with her father about her love life. That had been a mother and daughter thing. He wondered if Poppy would talk to him more now. For the present she said no more.

Later he phoned Steve Blount. Aunt Betty was in a residential care home a few miles from Oakmere. She had not been hard to find because of her unusual name. She was now eighty-seven years old, a little frail, but in full command of her faculties, according to the Matron that Steve had spoken to. At first, he said, Aunt Betty wanted nothing to do with him, but he had persisted and ultimately, she had agreed to see her nephew.

"She does not sound exactly gracious," Steve commented. "She has agreed provisionally, but you will have to agree a date and time through the Matron. She wants at least a week's warning."

Frank smiled into his phone. "Sounds as though she hasn't changed much. My daughter, Poppy, wants to come with me, but it might be wise not to tell Aunt Betty until we get there."

Poppy lost no time setting up a week's leave four weeks ahead. Frank called the Farmers Arms and booked rooms. He spoke to the Matron at Felthurst Residential Home. She sounded polite and well organised and said she would "catch Mrs Kristinin at a good moment" and arrange things. She took contact details. There was nothing to do but wait.

The tree planting seemed to have brought to an end one chapter of his life, but Frank still wanted to return to his earliest years. Whatever the truth about is mother's short, tragic life, he needed to discover it. Once that was complete, maybe he would feel ready to think about the future. At the moment the future yawned before him like a dark chasm into which he was reluctant to leap.

Chapter eight

Kylie was an excellent worker. With her help Frank emptied the room Louise had used as an office. He asked Janice to take any papers relating to the school, if they were worth saving. The rest he took to the bottom of the garden to the incinerator. Then he repainted the room for no reason other than to keep busy. He spent a lot of time in the garden on fine days. At half-term Kylie brought her children with her. They were in awe of Frank until he invited them to join him in the garden, where he ran races with them, played hide and seek, and allowed them to pick apples from one of the trees. They were especially interested in the garden pond and all the insects and creatures that lived in it. Soon their shyness faded. When they all trooped indoors and drank soft drinks, Kylie was amazed. She told the children to "thank Mr Whitaker" before thanking him herself. The house felt even more empty after that.

Frank continued to ponder what to do with the house. It was silly to hang on to the place, he told himself, but selling it would not only mean losing the house with so many memories in every room and every corner, including the attic, it would also mean leaving his precious garden. He loved the space as much as the trees, the shrub, and the flowers. Just to look at them gave him satisfaction and a sense of achievement and peace. He and Louise had worked together here as the trees developed from small plants into mature trees. Poppy had spent hours playing, growing like the trees. Leaving the garden would be impossibly difficult and would mark an abrupt and brutal break from the past thirty years.

He was in such a state of uncertainty when the time came to head back to Oakmere. He entrusted the keys to Kylie, though Jack and Iris would turn lights on and off as they had before. He drove to Oakmere on a Thursday. Poppy was driving separately and would meet him there. She was taking a week's leave before she began her new job. Frank arrived first and was once again sitting in the same, shabby chair when Poppy joined him. Jeremy, pleased to see them both, served them tea and sandwiches.

"I'm assuming the little restaurant in Orchard Street is still open," said Frank, smiling at his daughter. "The sandwiches are fine here, but I don't think it would be a good idea to eat in the bar."

They decided to eat early and the couple in the restaurant remembered them. Afterwards they returned to the Farmers Arms and headed for the bar.

"It's the wandering' star!" Phil greeted them from the back of the room where the Men's Shed group was gathered. "Come and join us!"

"I'm with my daughter," said Frank, "sorry."

"Don't be daft," said Phil, "I meant both of you."

"I thought this was a Men's Shed."

Phil laughed. "Only because we don't bring our wives," he said. "We don't have anything against women in principle, especially young, attractive ones, eh boys?"

There were cries of assent and more invitations. Poppy, amused, took her seat in the Windsor chair and Frank found room next to Steve Blount. Everybody seemed to be talking at once.

"So, what brings you back to the dead centre of the universe?" Pat asked. "It can't be the beer. We're all agog."

"Unfinished business, family stuff," said Frank. He was not prepared to say more even to this cheerful bunch of welcoming men. They took the hint and changed the subject.

"Didn't your dad say you were an air hostess?" someone asked. Poppy told them a little about her work.

"This place must seem very dull," said Gordon.

Poppy said she liked what she had seen of Oakmere. She explained that her job was not all glamour. She had to deal with passengers who fell ill, look after children. She said that many travellers were afraid of flying. Sometimes they drank too much and she had to clear up the mess.

"That can happen here at times," said Pat with a meaningful grin. He was looking at Frank. There was loud laughter before Doc asked politely if Poppy had been given any nursing training. Frank gave him a grateful smile.

It was a jolly evening. When Frank and Poppy said goodnight and were leaving, Steve followed them as far as the door.

"Good luck tomorrow," he said. "I suspect you'll need it. The Matron is pleasant enough, but Mrs Kristinin sounds like something of a Tartar, even at eighty-seven"

"Thank you for arranging it," Frank said. "I imagine you'll send me the bill at home."

"No charge," said Steve. "It has been an interesting brief."

"Gosh!" said Poppy. "That doesn't happen very often. My boyfriend's a lawyer. He'd be shocked there's no fee."

"It wasn't a normal job."

As they headed towards their rooms, Poppy commented, "I like them. Great bunch."

Frank turned into the drive of the Felthurst Residential Home with apprehension mingled with hope. By his side Poppy was curious to meet her Great Aunt. They left the car at the back of the large building where a signpost had directed them and they walked round to the large front door, feet crunching on the gravel. The grounds, Frank noted, were tidy but unimaginative in design, large areas of lawn interrupted by green shrubs and a profusion of laurel. A few planters along the front of the property would cheer it up immensely. Instead, it was a three-storey building in red brick, probably Victorian. The front door was open and they walked into a spacious hall, redolent of floor polish. On a table opposite the door a large flower arrangement stood, the only colour. A trim figure in a nurse's uniform stepped forward to greet them.

"Mr Whitaker?" She held out a hand. "I'm the Matron. Welcome to Feldhurst House. Your aunt is expecting you."

She led them to a door, tapped on it, then walked inside and announced them. Frank and Poppy walked in.

It was a big sitting room, furnished with armchairs, a table, several bookcases, and a television set in one corner. There was no bed;

there must be a separate bedroom. Great Aunt Betty was sitting in a wheelchair in a bay window. Pleasant though the room was, like the gardens it was lacking colour and quite dull. The chairs were covered in a faded chintz. The carpet was a very pale blue. The Matron withdrew quietly.

"Well, come in and sit down, you're making the place untidy," said Aunt Betty.

They did as they were told, finding seats that faced her. She was dressed in a silk shirt and a plain green skirt, half hidden by a rug. Her hair had recently been expertly done, but it was uniformly grey. She wore no perceptible make up. A glint of gold suggested she was wearing an expensive necklace. Her face was a little wrinkled, but less than might have been expected in someone of her age. Her lips were thin, her mouth a straight line. Her eyes were small and dark, scarcely visible at times.

"You are looking old, Frank," she said, "but I suppose it is a long time since I saw you."

"Over fifty years," he replied.

She sniffed. "That long? So, what brings you here now? Money, is it?"

"Money! Good heavens, no!"

"I can't think of any other reason. I haven't seen hide nor hair of you in half a century."

"And whose fault is that? You never answered my letters."

"What letters?"

"When I first moved to Berkshire at the age of seventeen, I wrote several letters. You never replied to any of them."

"Ah, those letters. I didn't really have anything to say to you."

Poppy watched the two of them. The age-old antagonism was obvious. Before she could say anything, however, Aunt Betty waved a bony hand in her direction and asked Frank, "Who is this?"

"Poppy's my daughter."

"Poppy! What sort of name is that I didn't know you had a daughter."

"I didn't know I had a great aunt," Poppy said.

For the first time there was the flicker of a smile on Betty's face. "Where's your wife?" She asked Frank.

"My wife died four months ago," he said, a spasm of pain on his features.

"Oh." She said nothing more, no word of understanding or sympathy. She had not changed, he thought. Nobody spoke for a few seconds.

"Well," she repeated, "why are you here?"

"You are the only person who can tell me anything about my mother," Frank said.

"Your mother? Madeleine? What on earth do you want to know about her?"

"You only ever told me that she died when I was three years old. You never said that she had taken her own life and to this day I have no idea why. I don't even know who my father was."

"Why do you need to know? It was all a long, long time ago."

"Don't you understand?" Frank was beginning to show his irritation. "She was my mother! I want to know about her! Surely even you can understand that!"

"Your mother was a sly, deceitful little girl."

Poppy could hardly believe her own ears and Frank was staring at his aunt with his mouth open in astonishment and anger.

"How can you say that? She was your sister!" Poppy exclaimed.

"Yes, she was my sister – unfortunately. But she got herself into trouble at the age of sixteen – or was it fifteen? And she always refused to name the father."

"I've been told she was raped!" Frank was beginning to lose his temper.

"Oh, that story! Yes, that was the tale she told everybody. Nobody believed her."

"Why on earth would she make up a story like that?" Poppy asked.

"You wouldn't understand. You're too young. Things have changed since then for the worst in my opinion. There's no sense of shame any more, all these unmarried mothers. No self-control, no discipline. And they expect the state to look after them, pay for their stupid mistakes, sometimes their deliberate choices."

"Are you saying," Poppy asked, "it never crossed your mind that she might be telling the truth?"

"Of course not! If she had been raped," said Aunt Betty, "she would have said something the day that it happened. She didn't say anything to anyone until she began to show."

"What if she was so scared of her parents that she daren't tell them she'd been attacked?"

"Rubbish! She was simply no better than she should have been. She was obviously covering for the boy."

Frank stood up. "I didn't come all this way to listen to you spread your malicious ideas about my own mother," he said, barely able to contain his anger.

Aunt Betty was unmoved. She shrugged. "Please yourself," she said.

Poppy felt almost as angry as her father but she held her ground as he turned abruptly and headed for the door.

"I didn't believe my father," she said, "when he told me about you. The only good thing you ever did for him, he said, was to take his mother in when she came to you for help. I suppose he should at least be grateful for that, though I can't understand why you took her in, if you thought so little of her."

"He certainly should be grateful. I had problems of my own. The last thing I needed was a sixteen-year-old mother intruding. She was obviously pregnant."

"Yet you took her in."

"Again, you don't understand what things were like in those days. We had standards. We understood the meaning of responsibility and duty. I could not send her away. How old are you?"

"Thirty-one."

"I was nearly that age myself, married to a very selfish old man. He was a miser, completely self-centred. He treated me like his personal slave. My marriage ring was like a shackle."

"But you stayed with him for years and years!"

"I keep telling you, we had standards, you don't understand what things were like in those days. When you got married, it really was for life. We made vows before God."

"I understand that but, if he was such a monster, how come he let you take Madeleine in?"

"It caused even more bitterness between us," Aunt Betty admitted. "And when the silly girl threw herself off that bridge..."

"Is that really how you see her, a silly girl?" Poppy was horrified. "She was obviously at the end of her tether. Are you really that unsympathetic even now?"

"It was the most selfish thing anyone could do," Aunt Betty replied tartly. "She left a three-year-old without a mother or a father and her older sister was lumbered with his care. I didn't want somebody else's child, someone else's bastard. I wanted a child of my own, something I dreamed of for years, something my miserable husband refused to do anything about."

Poppy was staring at her. She was trying to take in the information.

"Your perception of all this seems horribly warped," she said. "You make yourself sound like the victim. It was your sister who died and it was your nephew, my father, who was left an orphan."

"I looked after him as best I could."

"He says you never even showed him any affection. Didn't you care if he was happy or unhappy?"

"Don't you try lecturing me, young lady! I was desperate for a child of my own but I was lumbered with my sister's bastard to bring up, somebody else's child. We never even found out who the father was. And I never had a child of my own."

"I cannot understand why you didn't adopt him."

"Adopt him? I paid enough for my sister's sins without that, and in any case my husband would never have agreed."

It was Poppy's turn to leave. She stood up, made a helpless gesture with her arms, and left the room. Aunt Betty spoke to her retreating back. "I like people who say what they think. Good for you" As she crossed the hallway, the Matron smiled at her and said, "Thank you for coming. I'm sure it will have done Mrs Kristinin the world of good."

Poppy could find nothing to say. She walked round to the back of the house where Frank was sitting in the car staring at the uninteresting grounds. She got in beside him, reached over awkwardly to put her arms round his neck and hold him. After a while he disengaged himself, wiped tears from her face without saying a word, and drove off. A few miles on the other side of the village they found a local beauty spot near a river. They parked and sat for a while, not speaking for some time.

"What an awful old woman!" Poppy said at last. "She has left me with such a bad taste in my mouth. I wish we hadn't come."

"I'm sorry I walked out and left you," Frank said. "I simply couldn't take any more, although I didn't get the answers to half the questions."

"She told me quite a lot after you left," said Poppy. "Do you know, there were moments when I even felt just a teeny bit sorry for her."

"Sorry for Aunt Betty? After all she said about her own sister? Do you realise she didn't once say that she was sorry to hear your mother –" He could not complete the sentence.

"Your aunt is every bit as awful as you remember her, but I don't think I've ever met anyone so deeply unhappy."

"Unhappy? I suppose that's true, but maybe it's a case of you reap what you sow."

"Maybe. I think I managed to ask some of the questions you wanted answers to."

"Oh?"

And Poppy related the gist of the conversation to her father.

Driving home later, Frank was unable to rid himself of the memory of the brief, acrimonious meeting with his aunt. It clung to him, like a bad smell that had permeated his clothes. It was so severe that the moment he let himself in to his house he went straight to his bedroom, took a shower, dressed in clean clothes before proceeding to the kitchen. He loaded the washing machine and made himself some tea. Only then did he notice the flowers which Kylie had set on the table. Beside them was a small pile of letters and a colourful sheet of paper. He looked at it and smiled. It had been Welcome home", in several colours. The letters were of low interest. He must remember to order some special biscuits or sweets which he could keep as treats. This single act of kindness cheered him considerably but his thoughts kept returning to the fifteen minutes he had spent with his aunt. He had learned a little more about his mother's death, but at considerable cost to himself. He was especially disturbed by the strength of his own distaste, bordering on hatred. The image of the old woman's face presented itself repeatedly, an image which aroused such an intensity of feeling that he felt ashamed, yet he was unable to control it. By habit, by nature he was a kindly man. He liked and trusted most people that he met. This was a new experience and he could not undo it. It was as though he had been bitten by a venomous snake whose venom threatened to spread throughout his system.

His phone rang. It was Poppy.

"How are you? I don't think the meeting with Aunt Betty did you much good, did it? I was worried about you. At least you don't need to see her again."

"No, thank God for that! I don't think I've ever been quite so angry and upset. Thank you for being there, Poppy. I don't know how you managed it, but you extracted some important information. That's something, I suppose."

"Even the information was truly shocking. The best thing you can do is forget it."

"I wish I could. I'll try."

"Actually, I wanted to phone you anyway. There may be something positive to come out of all this after all."

"What's that?"

"I have never discussed my love life with you."

"No, you haven't. You are an adult and, if you wanted to talk to me about such things, I thought you would. I just respected your privacy. Mind you, your mother usually passed on important news about boyfriends."

"I had no secrets from Mummy. It's one of the reasons I miss her so badly."

"What has this got to do with our visit to Aunt Betty?"

"You hardly know Martin. He and I have been in a relationship for more than a year and it is serious."

"This is where I'm supposed to say I'm happy for you, isn't it?"

Poppy laughed. "Yes. The fact is that I'd like to bring him down for the weekend. It's time the two have you got to know one another better."

"This weekend?"

"If that's okay with you."

"Of course, it is. I look forward to it."

"There's more."

"More?"

"I told you meeting Aunt Betty was involved or at least connected."

"I don't understand."

"She reminded me I'm thirty-one years old. Well, she asked how old I was. But she also said how all her life had been ruined because she wanted children and never had them. She didn't see you in that way."

"I still don't quite understand what you are saying."

"Martin and I want to settle down together and start a family."

Frank was stunned.

"Daddy, are you still there?"

"You've taken my breath away," he said.

"Are you shocked? I know we are not married but as good as."

"Poppy, I am delighted! I just hope Martin can make you happy."

"Oh, he will. He really is a lovely man."

"He'd better be. If he's going to father my grandchildren, he'll have me to answer to!"

It was Poppy's turn to be amused. "You'll get on famously," she said. "And I'm so pleased that you aren't too shocked at the idea of becoming a grandfather."

"You're not pregnant yet, are you?"

"Not yet, no, but that sad, old woman and her experience reminded me that my body clock is ticking. I want children."

"Well, this has given me something new to think about. I shall look forward to seeing you both."

He rang off. More, than anything, he wanted to talk to Louise about this. He walked out into the garden they had made and felt he had been abandoned. At the far end of the garden, he sat on an old chair next to his compost bins. He was facing a mature apple tree, one of the very first trees they had planted together. He began to talk to her as though she were sitting next to him. He talked about Poppy and her plans to start a family. He talked about Martin, the young man he had met only briefly. He trusted his daughter's judgement, but he remained anxious. He had no religious convictions, but he remained uncertain about a relationship that was not formalised. For the moment, he told his wife's invisible presence, he could do nothing but wait. It would be great if Poppy carried out her plan. He remembered watching her as a small child playing in this garden. Many of the trees had been only saplings at that time. Now they were mature. He took pleasure in watching and hearing Kylie's children playing in the same area, but it would be so much nicer if he had grandchildren of his own. He stopped talking. He knew there was no one to hear him, but he felt strangely better to have spoken out loud.

Martin was a handsome, broad shouldered young man, approximately the same age as Poppy He dressed in expensive casual wear. Frank prepared a tray of coffee and biscuits which Poppy carried out to the terrace.

"I suppose," said Frank, grinning, "I should be asking you questions about your prospects. Isn't that what I'm supposed to do?"

Poppy laughed. "Sorry, Martin, I haven't told my father anything about you."

"Why? Surely, you're not ashamed of me?" The wide grin that accompanied this showed that it was not to be taken seriously.

"Poppy has always confided in her mother," Frank explained. "I didn't mind. She told me all I needed to know. Mind you, I have no idea what you do. Do you work for the same company?"

"Yes, I do. I am a lawyer. It's pretty boring stuff most of the time. It does pay well, I suppose. I spend my time drawing up or checking contracts. I imagine gardening is far more rewarding."

Frank laughed. "Poppy has at least told you that I'm a gardener, has she?"

Martin nodded. "Have I got it wrong?"

"No, I am a gardener, it's true, but I don't spend my time in a pair of old corduroy trousers tied up with string dabbling in this soil, not these days."

"Daddy is the Head Gardener for the Borough," Poppy explained. "He's in charge of the team that looks after all the parks and gardens, including cemeteries."

"I hope I haven't given the wrong impression," Martin said. "I hope you didn't think I was making judgements about your job. I didn't even think about it until I got here. Any father of Poppy's would obviously be a great bloke."

Frank and Poppy both laughed at this clumsy remark, as Martin turned red.

"Martin," Frank said, "I know what you're saying. Thank you. Shall we talk about something else?"

Martin took a sip of his coffee and recovered his equanimity. "This is a beautiful garden," he said. "How big is it? It looks as if it goes on forever."

"It's about half an acre," Frank said. "We were very lucky to be able to buy when we did. It's on the edge of agricultural land as you'll see if we wander down to the end later. This was part of a field then. Louise, Poppy's mother, and I spent hours taming it, planting shrubs and trees. Poppy will remember seeing us plant some of them. They look pretty good now. We get loads of fruit from the trees. I give nearly all of it away. The vegetable patch is tucked out of sight down there on the left. There's never a shortage of fresh vegetables. We were very proud of it."

"I've never had a proper garden," Martin admitted. "It must be very satisfying."

"Where do you live?"

"In a flat. There is no land with it."

Poppy said, "We are negotiating the purchase of a small house. We both have savings and good jobs. We want to make a proper start in a new place."

"It's a pity you both work so far away," said Frank. "You could have moved in here. There's plenty of room."

"I don't think it would be a good idea really," Poppy said. "You would probably soon get fed up with having us hanging about, making a noise, bringing in all our friends."

"Well, it's true as I get older I value my peace and quiet, but you can have too much of a good thing, you know."

They strolled down the garden until they reached the end where the old chair stored by the compost bins. Beyond the boundary fence large straw bales were dotted across a large field.

"You certainly did well to buy this place," Martin said. "People will pay a fortune for all this privacy."

Poppy gave him a sharp look. All at once he looked embarrassed. "I'm sorry," he said, "I didn't mean –."

"You're right," Frank said. "We were extremely fortunate to buy it in the first place. Mind you, it was quite a wilderness then. The two of us poured a great deal of love into this place, which is why I am very reluctant to think about setting up."

"Selling up? Why on earth would you do that?" Martin asked.

"You see the house. It's far too big for one person."

"But you have someone coming in twice a week to help," Poppy pointed out.

"Yes," but it's almost too much for her. I certainly don't need five bedrooms. There is a full-scale family bathroom which I never use because there is an ensuite in our bedroom that was your mother's pride and joy. And downstairs there are two – yes, two drawing rooms. I occasionally sit in the smaller one to watch television, but I spend nearly all my time in the kitchen. We had that converted into a kitchen-diner. No, there is too much space. Come on, let's go back, and I'll show you around the mansion." They headed back towards the house. "Oh, and don't forget," Frank added, "there is a large attic which I have boarded over and, in the garden, I have a greenhouse and a large, potting shed. And, when I said two drawing rooms, I didn't mention the conservatory."

Described like that, the property did seem very large, Poppy admitted to herself, but she knew how much Frank loved the place and it would always be associated in her own mind with wonderful thoughts of growing up with both her parents. To lose the property was unthinkable.

The weekend went well. Frank had become an accomplished cook over the years and he had prepared a mildly exotic lunch which they ate in the kitchen. Martin was impressed. He had expected they would go out for the meal. After a while the conversation became less stilted and Poppy who had approached the weekend with mild apprehension, relaxed as the two men became more at ease with one another. She was relieved. She cared for both of them.

Frank wanted to know more about the house they were buying together. They were full of enthusiasm and explained what they hoped to do. Frank watched them, conscious of the bond between them and the excitement they clearly felt at starting out on a life together. They did not speak of marriage and Frank was careful to say nothing, but he would have preferred them to marry. Among other reasons he detested the very idea of referring to one or other as a "partner." "Husband" and "wife" were perfectly good labels. They also imply a degree of security. If one or the other were to be incapacitated or even die, remote though he hoped such eventualities were, the survivor might be left with a legal tangle. However, he kept these thoughts hidden.

They shared a pot of tea and a cake which Frank had also made, then they left. Frank waved goodbye and returned to a house which felt emptier than ever. He went into the greenhouse and watered the plants. At last, he went back indoors and turned on the television to watch "Country File."

Chapter nine

As the weeks passed Frank grew accustomed to his routine. Twice a week Kylie came to do the basic housework. After a while it became obvious that four hours a week were not enough. It was a big house. Frank thought about it. He was not a mean man, but he was concerned with living within his means. He had drawn on his savings to make several excursions to Sussex. He had no regular salary payments until he returned to his post at the end of his year off. He simply had to undertake any additional housework himself. Shopping and cooking were activities he did not mind. He was perfectly capable of using a vacuum cleaner and a duster, though he sometimes smiled at the thought that he was merely moving the dust from one place to another. He was coping but the time he spent in the house was time he could have spent in the garden and the greenhouse. He sometimes felt frustrated, and thoughts of moving continued to cross his mind and be dismissed.

During the long, summer holidays Kylie brought her children with her and Frank grew fond of them both. He took them out to the garden and joined them in play or got them to help on the vegetable patch. Kylie always left with a bag full of homegrown produce, fresh fruit, and vegetables which she appreciated. She was, Frank soon learned, living on very little money. He suggested that she could possibly work more hours, and was surprised to learn that the time she could spend working and the money she could earn were limited. Too many hours could result in her benefit payments being cut or stopped altogether.

A phone call from Poppy one evening interrupted his routine. "Daddy," she said, "I hope you are free next Friday."

"I'll have to consult my diary," Frank replied with dry humour. "What's happening?"

"We'd like to show you the new house. Can you get here for 11 o'clock?"

"I should think so. I'll look forward to it."

He decided to travel by train to avoid problems with parking. It would be interesting to see the new house. Poppy had already told him it had three bedrooms. She and Martin had spent a great deal of time already sorting furniture and personal possessions from their separate flats. Poppy had shared a flat with her two friends, so had very little furniture to worry about, but she had accumulated lots of smaller items – clothes, books, DVDs, various electronical gadgets. Martin had completely furnished his flat. It was quite small, but he had several items of furniture. Frank was quietly amused at the air of excitement which accompanied any discussion about the proposed move.

He caught an early train and took a taxi from the station. Poppy greeted him with a huge hug and an unusual sense of excitement. Strange, Frank thought. She had taken great care with her appearance, even greater than usual. The viewing was obviously important to her.

"Where is Martin? "he asked.

"He's meeting is there."

Frank was surprised when the doorbell rang. "That'll be the cab," said Poppy.

"Aren't you driving?"

"Not this morning."

They climbed into the taxi which drove through the busy streets for five minutes. Poppy had taken Frank's hand and was squeezing it. She seemed strangely nervous. He looked at her. She looked back at him with a wide, happy smile, her eyes dancing. It seemed quite extraordinary that she should be so excited. He smiled back as the taxi drew to a halt. They were still in the middle of town. Frank stepped out and handed Poppy to the pavement and turned to pay the driver.

"All paid, guv," the driver said and turned to check his mirror before pulling away.

"Where are we going?" Frank asked, but Poppy laughed and pulled him by the hand up a broad set of steps that led to a large building. At the top of the steps double doors stood open. Frank entered with his daughter, bewildered.

"This way," she said, still with laughter in her voice. She led him up a wide staircase. Here, a woman in a smart, business suit waited. "Welcome!" she said. "Dead on time! Everything is ready. The groom is waiting."

Frank, nonplussed, opened his mouth but had no time to speak before the woman opened the door for them. Frank was speechless. Poppy had somehow managed to position herself on his right as they walked to the front of the large room. Martin was standing there, looking with open admiration at his bride.

The ceremony which followed was short and formal. Poppy had brought her two flatmates as witnesses as well as her father. Martin had also brought two young men, one of whom was his best man.

"I now pronounce you man and wife," said the Registrar. "You may now kiss the bride."

The witnesses clapped. Frank added his signature as a witness to the register, kissed his daughter and shook her new husband by the hand.

"We are all going to have a meal together," Martin explained, "then we shall show you the house. It is now ours. I hope you aren't too shocked by all this, Frank. It was mostly Poppy's idea to surprise you. Neither of us wanted a fuss"

"It certainly was a surprise. It was also a bit naughty. I couldn't look for a wedding present for you. I wish you both all the happiness in the world."

"You came, that's all we wanted," Poppy said.

"I am truly pleased for you," Frank said. He was far too emotional to say anything else, except to take both her hands in his and add, "Mrs Fairburn." He was asking himself what Louise would have made all this. Wouldn't she have preferred a full-blown wedding with flowers and champagne? He did not know, but he knew she would have been as pleased as he was. He was in a daze for the rest of the afternoon. The best man gave an amusing little speech and Frank found it difficult to respond. Thoughts of his humiliating performance at the tree planting made him steel himself. His sentiments, however, were so sincere that the little group listened with respect. He even managed to raise a laugh or two.

Afterwards the entire party climbed into two taxis and drove to the new house in the suburbs. It was an older house, probably built in the thirties. It was unremarkable, but it would be home. Poppy was obviously happy with it. She and Martin explained to their friends some of the plans they had to redecorate, possibly extend at the back. While they talked, fuelled by excitement and champagne, Frank wandered out into the garden. It all looked a little tired, but people had lived and loved here and it had a history of its own.

He felt Poppy's arm slip through his. "It's all right, don't you think?" she said.

"It's fine," he said. "The two of you will be happy here."

"Thank you for being here today," she said.

He squeezed her hand.

"And we'll need you to redesign the garden," she said.

"What if I make it my wedding present?"

"That would be great. It's not as big or grand as yours, of course."

"What matters," he said, "is that you are happy here. I'm still in shock. I am probably talking nonsense, but I can't get used to seeing you walk out of my life even to marry the man you love."

"Martin isn't replacing you," she said. "I'm still your daughter and you're still my father. Marrying Martin doesn't change that."

Neither of them said what was in their minds, how Louise should have been there. They stood for a while, holding on to the moment until Martin came out and they returned to the party.

On the train journey home later, Frank struggled to take in the day's events. He knew this was an important change not only for his daughter but also for their relationship. From now on Martin had the awesome responsibility of looking after her in the same way as he had cared for his own wife. Poppy would need to concern herself with Martin as Louise had loved him. It was a situation he could not quite grasp as yet. But, underlying all this turbulence was the steadying thought that they were officially man and wife. However sparse the wedding had been – and there had not even been a bouquet for the bride – they had chosen to formalise their relationship and he was glad. He wondered just how much Poppy would confide in him in future. Since Louise's death they had been closer. Now the intimacies would be shared with her new husband. This was turning into a year of changes, of endings, of partings. He wondered if, from all these unexpected, disruptive changes he could somehow find new beginnings. Somehow, he had to do so.

The autumn began crisp and dry. As was his custom, Frank drank an early cup of tea before spending an hour in the garden. Other people, he sometimes observed, went on a run to take exercise, but he preferred to do something more productive. He finished clearing out the greenhouse and lit a smoke bomb to fumigate it then left quickly leaving all the doors and windows firmly closed. It was Tuesday, one of Kylie's days, but the children would be safely in school. He made his way back indoors and washed his hands and sat down with a cup of tea in the kitchen. He heard Kylie let herself in by the front door. He waited but she did not look into the kitchen to say hello as he expected. Curious, he left the table and stepped into the hall. Kylie had dropped her coat and bag on the floor and was sitting on the stairs, bent over, her head in her hands. She looked up momentarily when she heard him come in, then looked away hurriedly but not before he caught a glimpse of her face. She was crying.

"Kylie," he said, "what's the matter? Are you ill?"

"No," she said. Her voice was muffled by the tissue she was holding to her face.

"So, what's the matter? Whatever it is, you shouldn't be sitting here, you'll get your death of cold. Come into the kitchen where we can talk."

"I'll be all right," she said, getting to her feet. "I'm sorry."

"Kitchen!" he commanded.

She was still avoiding his eyes but she did as he said.

"Sit down," Frank said, pointing out a chair for her. "Have a cup of tea."

He poured her a cup of tea and put half a dozen biscuits on a plate. She said nothing but drank the tea gratefully. She ate the biscuits as though she were hungry. She must have missed breakfast, Frank thought. He refilled her cup.

"I am sorry," she repeated. "Thank you for the tea. I feel better now."

"What has happened? What's the matter? It's not the children, is it?"

"The children? No, they are all right – well, for now, anyway."

"What does that mean?" Frank was alarmed.

"We are being kicked out of our house."

"What do you mean, kicked out?"

"I had a letter from the landlord this morning giving me one month's notice. We have nowhere to go. It's a pretty awful place, I know, but it's almost impossible to find anywhere to rent, at least anything I can afford."

"Can't you get housing benefit or something?"

"Yes, but it's just about impossible to find anywhere decent to accept housing benefits as payment."

"Surely your landlord can't just throw you out when you have nowhere to go, can he?"

"Theoretically no, but he's saying he's going to live in the place himself. As if he would! It's small, damp and not really fit for anyone to live in. The windows leak and the kitchen walls are always covered in mould, no matter how often I clean them with bleach."

"It doesn't sound suitable for bring up the children there."

"It's not! Of course, it's not. I know it, but what am I to do? I can't afford anything else."

"Maybe," Frank said, "I should have employed you for more than two days a week."

"You have been very kind," said Kylie. "Giving me a job like this has been a lifeline for me. But even if you had offered me more hours, it wouldn't really help. If I work more than sixteen hours a week, they simply stop my benefits."

Frank looked at her, beginning to understand her sense of helplessness.

"Anyway," she said, "I shouldn't be burdening you with all these problems. I'd better get on with my work. Thank you for the tea. You really are very kind. I appreciate it."

"Judging by the way you tucked into those biscuits," Frank said, "it looked as though you must've missed breakfast."

"I always make sure the children are properly fed." She sounded defensive.

"I'm sure you do. What about you?"

"I manage." She turned towards the door. Frank watched her go then sat for a long time, thinking. He liked the girl. He had watched her with her children and she was clearly a loving mother, something he had never experienced. He had realised that she had very little money to live on. She had always been so grateful for the gifts of fruit and vegetables. It dawned on him for the first time just how important those gifts must have been. Times were hard for many people. Working families as well as unemployed people were having to go to food banks. Kylie would probably have been in the same situation without his fruit and vegetables. As for her housing situation, that sounded desperate. He had never personally suffered accommodation problems. He and Louise had bought this big house cheaply through a combination of good luck and connections with the right people. They had worked very hard to turn it into a home where they planned to bring up their children, although, sadly, they had only one, Poppy. Kylie would probably make her way later that morning to the council offices and the Housing Department. But the Council would be very unlikely to help, according to what he understood. Ever since the decision to sell off council housing, the pressure had grown. Councils had not been allowed to build more replacements. People like Kyle were left homeless or living in expensive and unsuitable accommodation. Kylie would probably end up in one room in a rundown hotel somewhere.

He opened the door and called, "Kylie!" She appeared in the hallway again.

"Forget about the cleaning for the moment," he said "come back into the kitchen."

She followed him.

"What time do you have to pick up the children?" he asked.

"A quarter past twelve," she said

"Right, that gives us a good couple of hours."

She stared at him, not comprehending.

"I think I might have an answer to your immediate problem," he said. "It's staring me in the face. This house is much too big for one man on his own. If push came to shove, I could manage with this one room and my bedroom. I even have a mini-bathroom attached to the bedroom. I employ you two days a week to come here, even though that isn't enough to clean all the rooms. I could easily employ you for five days a week, but you can't do that without losing benefits. It's all absolutely stupid."

Kylie was looking at him, trying to understand what he was saying.

"Now, I'd say we get along quite well together, wouldn't you?"

She nodded, wary now. She liked Mr Whitaker, but what he seemed to be driving at was surely not what she thought. He had lost his wife just a few months ago. He was not going to suggest she moved in with him, was he? Did he really think she was so desperate she would go to bed with him in return for somewhere to live? He was old enough to be her father! She began to stiffen with distaste at the very prospect.

"As you know," Frank continued, completely unaware of what Kylie was thinking, "there are five good bedrooms in this house. There is also a perfectly good, family bathroom which I never use. Downstairs there are two drawing rooms and the conservatory. In short, there are acres of space which I don't need. You, on the other hand, will shortly be without somewhere to live. There is only one, major snag."

Kylie was still unsure where the suggestion was leading.

"There is only one kitchen," he said.

"I don't know what on earth you are talking about," said Kylie. "Why would you want another kitchen? This one is lovely."

"I'm not explaining this very well, am I? Bear with me and I'll try to explain. I've been thinking for a long time now what to do with this house. I don't really want to sell it. Although it's too big, I love it and it contains so many memories I'd find it hard to move out. And I love the garden even more. So, here is my suggestion: instead of working for me just two days a week, you work five days. I know about the problem of payments and benefits." He held up a hand before she could say anything. "Instead of paying you a proper wage for five days a week, you work for me in return for free accommodation plus pocket money for the time being until the

Council can find you suitable accommodation. You, Ollie, and Emma will have the use of two of the bedrooms. My bedroom and the one that used to be Poppy's, as it happens are at this end of the house. Downstairs, you, and the children will have one of the two drawing rooms and share with me the conservatory. The so-called family bathroom would be yours for you and the children exclusively. I simply don't need it. The only problem remaining, as I said, is that there is only one kitchen."

Kylie was staring at him, hardly believing what she heard.

"The main thing is," Frank continued, "would you be prepared to do five days a week? Oh, I forgot to say you would all be welcome to use the garden, of course, and I will be responsible for the running costs and food. As I say, we seem to get on quite well, and I like the children and they seem to like me. At the very least it might solve your problems until you could find somewhere else to live. Sharing the kitchen might require some careful planning. I am very fussy about the kitchen. Cooking is my principal hobby. But, as I say, it depends on what you think."

"I can't expect you to share this lovely home with me and my children!"

"Do you know, one of the things that I discussed with Poppy, when we talked about the size of this house, was the possibility that we could house refugees here. Well, in a sense, you are refugees yourselves."

"I don't know what to say." Kylie was crying again. "Of course, I would love to accept! I would be mad to think otherwise. But – "

"But?"

"This is all so quick! I don't think it's fair on you. I'd love to say yes, this is the answer to all my problems all in one go. But what if tomorrow or next week you change your mind?"

"I suppose that's a good point. It's not very likely. The only room for argument, literally, would be the kitchen. The important thing is do you agree in principle to all this?"

"Of course, I do."

Kylie went back to her house, hardly daring to believe her employer would not change his mind. She said nothing to her children. She was in such a state, however, that she abandoned her original plan of going to the Housing Department. This, she thought, was all one wonderful dream that would disappear the following morning. She lay awake most of the night, her mood alternating between ecstasy and reality. When Oliver asked if she was all right, she said she had slept badly. She walked them to the school and waved goodbye before returning to the large house. She let herself in as usual and looked into the kitchen briefly. She waited for Frank to ask her in so that he could tell her he had changed his mind, but he was busy on his phone and merely waved a greeting. She returned to her normal duties.

While Kylie had been trying to keep control of her hopes and fears, Frank had called Poppy to tell her what he planned.

"Are you sure this is right for you?" Poppy asked. "I don't know Kylie very well, of course. She seems very pleasant and you have said that she is very honest and so on. But it's a big step, sharing your home with her and her children."

"I know. But I am sure this is the right thing to do. You know what I think about the size of this place. You also know how attached to it I am. I'd like to think it's somewhere you and Martin will always be welcome. Mind you, if you start producing children in any quantity, I may regret her lack of bedroom space in future."

Poppy laughed. "I dare say we could find ways round that," she said, "even if it means staying in a travel lodge or camping on the lawn Just so long as you are sure that you are doing the right thing."

"Well, I intend to go ahead," her father said. "Among other things it will mean the children have a more secure childhood. I know from experience how important that is."

"So do I, thanks to you and Mummy."

"We're talking as though this will be a permanent arrangement," frank said, entering a sudden note of caution. "You never know, Kylie may find somewhere more permanent in a matter of week."

"I don't believe all this is happening," Kylie repeated. "I just don't believe anyone could take all this trouble just for me."

"It's not just for you," Frank said. "It's for you and Ollie and Emma, of course, but it's also for me. "

"I can't see what you're going to get out of it."

"Well, I don't need to worry about the house any more for a start, do I? You're going to be full-time sorting that out. You are the one going to be giving up four days a week. I will be out off doing my own work. And it means I can come back to my own home."

"Something is bound to go wrong. This is just a dream. And it's all happened so fast."

Frank looked at her with a smile. "Exciting, isn't it?"

Kylie could not reply.

"Call the kids," he said. "They might as well polish off the rest of this cake."

Kylie was aware just how much pride Frank took in the kitchen. She did her utmost to use it only when essential, but she still had to feed her children. They managed the process generally well. Frank's habit of rising early and working in the garden was fine, although there were occasional, minor problems on wet mornings. The situation was also eased on two occasions when Frank absented himself for two short periods. Once autumn arrived and it was time to prune or tidy away much of the fresh growth in the garden, it was also a good time to visit Poppy and Martin and to set to work on their garden. Kylie and the children were left to occupy the house. Kylie was proud to be trusted with such a responsibility and promptly set about spring-cleaning the less used rooms. She had Frank's phone number. Frank warned Jack and Iris, too, and they were ready to help in an emergency.

Poppy and Martin were out at work all day. Frank was happy to work undisturbed. There was a lot to do, starting with the removal of some of the existing shrubs and the remains of a poor lawn. He hired the appropriate equipment and a large skip and set to work. It was years since he had engaged in such physical labour and he was grateful to relax every evening in a bath. He was very stiff for the first week, but he realised how unfit he had become after several years spent part-time in the office. As he expected, seeing the transformation of the tired space gave him great satisfaction. It was especially enjoyable the second week. By then the ground had been cleared and flattened. He marked out a new path from the back door in a curve which made the garden seem much bigger. New shrubs and perennials were planted in beds which interrupted the area of new turf.

"Once the grass had had a chance to grow," he explained to the astonished and delighted Martin, "don't cut it too short at first. Let the roots join hands first. Make sure you keep it well watered."

There were no emergency calls from Kylie or from Jack. Frank phoned home twice, but all was well. He spent his time at work thinking of what he was doing and organising the delivery of turf and plants. He was enjoying himself.

Martin and Poppy took him out to dinner on the last night. They were very grateful for all he had achieved on his own in such a short time.

"Come May or June" Frank told them, "you'll be surprised how different it will all look – provided you keep up the waterings, that is. There's not too much maintenance, but you're going to need a lawnmower. I don't suppose you've got one, have you?"

"How soon will I need to start cutting the grass?"

"Not for a few weeks."

"Maybe," Poppy said, "you can help us choose one when you come for Christmas."

Frank had not thought about Christmas. Since the wedding he had not thought about any form of family gathering except for the time he was going to spend on the garden. Thoughts of Christmas were not altogether alluring. Like every other anniversary Christmas would force him to think about Louise and the times they had spent in the past. He dreaded thinking even for a moment about the day when Louise had died. He should in theory be ready to think of the more agreeable times, the birthdays, the holidays, the Christmases they had spent together. Now that two of the rooms at home – home is how he still thought of it – were occupied by Kylie and the children, a Christmas with Poppy and Martin would be very strange. He had not thought about the possibility that his daughter and son-in-law would want him to join them in their home, not his. This was already a very strange year. The worst part had undeniably been losing Louise, he had also chosen to take a year away from his customary job. The extraordinary and emotional memorial ceremony at the school had given him a great deal to think about. He had been very moved at the outpouring of affection it had provoked, even for him. Three other experiences had followed rapidly, his visit to Oakmere and meeting with his aunt, his decision not only to employ Kylie, but also to reorganise his much-loved home, and finally the completely unexpected marriage of his daughter.

"I hadn't thought about Christmas," he said, "but it would be a good idea, if you don't mind having me for a few days. I may not be very good company, that's the only thing."

Poppy looked at him. "In some ways it's going to be a sad time for me, too," she said. "I'm not sure I shall be completely ready to enjoy it. Perhaps we shall both have to hide away in a corner somewhere and weep on each other's shoulders. I just thought it was sort of symbolic or something, both of us trying to start anew. I've talked about this to Martin. He understands."

Martin nodded. "Just a quiet time," he said, "we'd like to invite my mother and father for Christmas Day, though, no parties, nothing like that. It could be good for you. And in any case," he added, "I need your advice on buying a new lawnmower."

"It's very good of you both," Frank said. "And I hope we can have an enjoyable time. I'm sure Louise would want us to."

He told Kylie when he got home.

"You can have the kitchen to yourselves," he said. "I'll stay until after New Year's Day. You can even have a bit of a party. We always used to decorate the drawing too. The decorations must all be in the loft. The children will enjoy helping."

Kylie had never had a tree to decorate. Christmas was a difficult time for her. She usually went without even the simplest luxuries to buy one or two extras, such as chocolate and ready-made mince pies. She hunted in charity shops for cheap toys. This Christmas would, she knew, be different, now she had wages coming in. They would be enough to buy not only a large chicken, but the ingredients to make her own mince pies. She had intended to ask if she could use the kitchen for the preparation. Now Mr Whitaker had told her she could even entertain friends if she wanted. She let the invitation go, however, relishing the prospect of celebrating Christmas with Ollie and Emma in a warm room, with a Christmas tree and a television set. No matter if the wind howled and rain or even snow beat against the windows, the three of them would be snug, warm, and safe. She could buy one or two new presents and treat herself to a small box of chocolates. It would be bliss. She wished she could buy a suitable present for Mr Whitaker, but she could not think of anything she could afford until she peered into his bathroom while he was out, and identified the brand of shaving cream he used. She bought a pack of aftershave and deodorant which she would wrap in bright paper. The children could make him cards. Suddenly Christmas was exciting, a happy time rather than a source of anxiety and guilt. Frank was surprised to hear her singing carols in November.

Janice rang him one evening around this time. "We haven't seen you for a while," she said. "It has been so busy, sorry. I wondered if you would like to come to our Nativity Play. You could watch Ollie and Emma. Ollie thinks the world of you."

"No thanks," said Frank. "It's nice of you to ask but…"

"Right you are. Ollie will be especially disappointed, though. He keeps us fully informed; you know. He tells us he and Emma have new beds. Are they taking up permanent residence?"

"Something like that. I'll be a bit more careful what I say when he's listening. The idea is that they can stay until they find a more permanent place of their own."

"Oh!" Janice paused for a moment before adding cautiously, "I hope you've thought this through, Frank "

"It's a no-brainer, Janice, I've got plenty of space. As for Ollie, I don't want him seeing me as a father figure."

"Too late for that, I'm afraid. Much better you than that rat of a real father."

"I don't know anything about Kylie's husband or ex-husband."

"I don't think they were ever married. The lived together about five years, I think. I believe he was a very rough chap. From things Ollie let drop, he used his fists a lot. Shortly after Emma was born, he was arrested for aggravated burglary. He's an addict. He was given eighteen months, I think, but he only served half that time. Emma was rehoused after that."

Frank whistled. "I didn't know any of this," he said.

"Maybe I should have told you before. It's all in the past now, and it's not my business. I just feel so sorry for the children – and for Kylie, of course."

Frank thought about the information. Maybe it was more unpleasant gossip. According to Janice the man was forbidden to make further contact with Kylie or the children. All the same, he wished it had been Kylie that told him about the ugly relationship.

Chapter ten

As he had expected, the ten days he spent with Poppy and Martin were a mixture of pleasure and pain. The pain of loss always lingered in the background. The muted celebrations in a different house could not override the memories of former Christmases. Frank pushed them to the back of his mind as far as he could, as did Poppy. The small party of five people on Christmas Day was agreeable and civilised but there was little spontaneous fun. By way of contrast Kylie took photographs of the Christmas tree and the happy faces of the children and sent them to Frank's phone. He was pleased for her, but his first sight of familiar decorations on the tree, decorations which had accumulated over the many years, caused unexpected pain. Poppy and Martin did their best to distract him. They drove out for a meal on New Year's Day. The food was marvellous. Poppy knew that her father was a very keen, amateur cook. She asked him how he and Kylie were getting on, sharing the kitchen. Frank admitted that it was going well so far. Kylie was meticulous about tidying up and putting things away

Frank's leave of absence expired in February. When he looked back over the year, it had not been restful in the least. The trip to Oakmere had failed to settle his mind: if anything, the discovery that his mother had taken her own life was worse than not knowing anything about her. Thoughts and reminders of Louise's death were still quite fresh. Poppy's sudden and quiet wedding was like an unexpected goodbye. He was no longer the major influence in her life. The tree planting ceremony at the school, now several months in the past, had been an extraordinary and generally uplifting experience, but it, too, had been a ceremony in which celebration of his wife's work was like a final, highly decorative exit stamp in a passport from his previous life. It marked the end of an era. The arrival of Kylie and the children was the most positive thing that had happened, but it had involved learning about the life of poverty she had experienced. It was good to have children back in the house even temporarily. He was especially pleased that they could enjoy the garden.

He had quite deliberately kept well away from the Council and especially his normal workplace. As February approached, he felt he had to brace himself to plunge back into the routine, most of which was administration these days. He had taken no interest in anything to do with council activity, not even staying in regular touch with his Deputy. The day finally arrived when he drove the short distance to his offices. Nothing much appeared to have changed. It was a slack time of the year, a time for repairs, for tidying up and cleaning. It was also a time to look at possible new plantings and to order new seeds. The vast majority of the propagation consisted of making cuttings rather than buying new stock.

He walked into the larger room where the workmen came to drink their tea and eat their sandwiches. All eight were there to welcome him back. He was touched by their welcome and chatted for a while before he entered his own office for the first time in twelve months. Bill, his Deputy, who had run the Department in his absence, followed him.

"You aren't going to enjoy the first day," he said.

"Probably not," said Frank," but I suppose I shall soon get used to it all again."

"I hope so. I've left the most important memo from the Treasurer on the top of the in tray. You are not going to like that one bit. I'm just very glad you're going to have to deal with it, not me."

Frank sat in the familiar chair and reached for the in tray. The memorandum in question was quite a long document. He scanned it quickly. The Finance Committee, it reported, had been severely affected by a 20% reduction in government funding for the coming year. A succession of such cuts over the past six years had obliged the Council to prune many of its services. The next year would be more than challenging, it would involve cuts that were going to hurt. After a great deal of deliberation, one such would affect the budget for the Parks and Gardens Department. Further savings of 20% were required. This, according to the Treasurer, could only be achieved by reducing the staffing level.

Frank looked through the departmental finances. He could see no way of reducing the budget other than doing as the Treasurer recommended. The Treasurer, however, would not have to face the individual who was going to lose his job. For a few minutes, his heart sinking, Frank thought about asking for early retirement. It would solve the budget problem, but he needed the income more than ever. He could not afford to abandon four years' income from his job until he was entitled to the state pension. It looked as though he would have to tell the youngest member of his team to look for another job. With one last throw of the dice, he drove to the main Council Office to speak directly to the Treas. It was all very professional and amicable, but it achieved nothing.

That evening he drove home feeling thoroughly dejected. He left the car at the front of the house and walked round to the garden entrance. It was quite dark but light from the kitchen spilled out onto the lawn, offering a warm welcome home on a cold evening. As he approached the glass doors, he heard a loud crash from inside the room, as though a piece of furniture had been knocked over. He ran the last two or three steps and pulled back the door.

A man in jeans and a denim jacket swung round to meet him.

"Who the hell are you?" asked the stranger. He was unshaven and wild eyed. He was a comparatively young man. Behind him, lying awkwardly and untidily on the floor, Kylie did not move Blood trickled from a corner of her mouth and her face was red. She appeared to have been struck. Cowering near her, Ollie and his sister were pressed against the wall, terrified.

"This is my house," Frank replied, "and I'm calling the police. Have you done this to Kylie?"

By way of reply the man reached out and grabbed one of the knives which Frank kept on the work surface, the blades embedded in a heavy block of wood. With this lethal weapon in his right hand the stranger took a step towards Frank, yelling at him with obscenities to put down his phone. Frank ignored the command, pressing 999. A voice asked, "Which service, police, fire, or ambulance?" But before Frank could reply the man lunged towards him, knife foremost. Frank had hooked his right foot round a wooden stool and he sought to defend himself by kicking the stool towards his attacker. It caught the man on the shin, causing him to stumble and fall, the knife slicing into Frank's left forearm. As he fell his head met the edge of the work surface. He fell awkwardly over wreckage of the stool and finished on his back. He lay still. There was a great deal of blood from the cut in Frank's arm. It ran down over his hand and dripped onto the floor tiles to make a small pool. Kiylie, dazed but coming round, cried out. Ollie was trembling, unable to move. His sister was shrieking.

"Kylie," Frank shouted, "tie him up."

Kylie cast about for something to use.

"Undo my belt and take it off me!" Frank ordered.

Reluctantly, Kylie did as she was asked. She managed to secure the man's arms behind his back, tying the worn leather as tightly as she could around his wrists. Frank, meanwhile, had grabbed a tea towel which he wrapped around his arm.

"Ollie!" he shouted to the boy, "Take your sister upstairs to the bathroom and bring me a towel to wrap round my arm."

The boy did as he was asked while Kylie did her best to staunch the flow of blood with two more tea towels. They were soon soaked.

"The police! Call them again!"

Frank had never felt range of such intensity. It was so strong that he did not at first feel the pain, although it was clearly a severe wound. Ollie returned with two towels, one of which Frank wound round his wounded arm. He prodded the supine figure with his foot.

"What in God's name was he doing here?" he asked.

"He was looking for money. It's Gus, the children's father. He's on drugs."

"You didn't invite him here, surely?"

"No. I don't know how he found us." The initial shock was beginning to wear off. It resolved itself into tears which ran over her swollen face. "Is he safe there? I tied him up as tightly as I could. It wasn't easy with the leather. What if he comes round?"

"If he so much as twitches," Frank said, "I'll kick his bloody head in."

He staggered as far as a chair as the pain surged all at once. He clutched his arm. Kiylie poured him a glass of water, stepping carefully to avoid the blood. He drank gratefully. The two children crept close to their mother and clung to her.

The front door bell rang and someone pounded on the door, then they heard footsteps as someone ran round the side of the house towards the glass doors. A large, uniformed policeman stepped inside.

"My God!" he exclaimed, as a second uniformed figure appeared behind him, a woman this time. Already the man was speaking into his radio. "We need backup and an ambulance. At least one injured man, possibly two. One man has suffered a knife wound."

The policewoman was checking that the children were all right before she turned her attention to Kylie.

"What happened here?" the man asked. "It's absolute carnage. Is all this blood yours?" He was speaking to Frank who merely nodded. The towel around his forearm was now soaked

"This man came here looking for money," Frank said. "He had attacked my housekeeper when I arrived and he went for me with a knife." He was finding it difficult to concentrate now.

"Who tied him up?"

"I did," said Kylie. "And I know him. His name is Gus Anstead."

"Anstead," the policewoman repeated. "Don't we know him?"

"Could be," said her colleague.

Outside came the sound of an ambulance siren. Twenty minutes of busy confusion followed. Jack and Iris had heard the ambulance and came to investigate just as a second police car turned up. They agreed to look after the two children while Kylie and Frank were taken into A and E. Gus had recovered consciousness and was taken to the police station where a police surgeon would look him over. The children were upset at being left behind, though Kylie explained she would come back as soon as the doctors let her go. Fortunately, Ollie and Emma knew Iris and Jack. They were treated to hot chocolate and wrapped up in rugs while they waited. When

Kylie returned three hours later, they were sound asleep, close together on a settee.

"You're all staying here until your place has been cleaned up," Iris insisted. "We've got a perfectly good spare bedroom."

But Kylie preferred to spend the rest of the night in an armchair, leaving the children undisturbed. Frank, his wound dressed and stitched, lay in a hospital bed with a catheter in his good arm, the lost blood being replaced by a saline drip.

He was released at midday and phoned for a taxi. He was still in his working clothes and without his belt. He was obliged to use his one good hand to prevent his trousers from falling down when he walked. He was halfway home before he realised he had no money with him. He never took his wallet to work. He explained to the taxi driver who found it funny. Frank was growing more and more irritable by the moment. Although he had his keys with him, it was decidedly awkward to open the front door, so he returned to the kitchen doors. Kylie was on her knees, scrubbing the last vestiges of the previous day's melee off the floor. Frank asked her to run upstairs to his room and retrieve his wallet to pay the driver. She did so without entering into a conversation. Frank took a seat until she returned, he was surprised just how tired he felt.

"I need some kind of a shower," he said. "I need to change my clothes. It's going to be difficult with one arm but I suppose I shall have to get used to it."

"Can you manage?" Kylie asked.

"I bloody well have to!" He seldom swore, so Kylie was taken aback as Frank made his way to the stairs and so to his room. The simple procedure of taking a shower while keeping his left arm dry made his irritation worse. It proved quite impossible to put on a shirt. He grabbed a bath robe, inserted his good arm into the sleeve, and draped the left side over his shoulder. Tying the belt one-handed was also impossible. He made his way back down to the kitchen and asked Kylie to help. Then he sat down at the table.

"Have you had anything to eat?" she asked.

"Not since breakfast."

"What can I get you?"

"Whatever it is, I have to eat it with just my right hand. I don't know, use your imagination." He was clearly still bad-tempered.

Kylie made some scrambled eggs with bacon. She cut up the toast and the bacon into small squares, the way she would feed a small child.

"I'll go and see the housing manager tomorrow," she said.

"What?"

"After all this," Kylie said, still busy at the cooker, "you won't want us around any longer. I understand that. I am so sorry."

"Kylie! What the hell are you talking about?"

"It's all my fault," she said. "The only reason Gus came here was by following me. He was looking for money to buy drugs with. If I hadn't been here, he wouldn't have followed me, and you wouldn't be sitting there with a bad arm."

"You are talking nonsense. It was then stupid, incompetent idiot who stabbed me, not you. You couldn't know he was coming here. As for looking for somewhere else to live, forget it for now. There's no hurry, Un fact, it looks as though I need someone here for the moment."

She put the plate of food in front of him. "Do you mean that?" she asked.

"Of course, I mean it!"

"You are the most forgiving man I have ever met. I shall never be able to repay this."

"I may have to teach you some culinary skills," Frank said. "If I can't do the cooking myself, I shall have to teach you some of my tricks."

"Well, I can manage scrambled eggs," Kylie said, perking up.

"Yes, I'm sorry I swore."

"I've heard a lot worse, and you've got plenty to swear about."

She had made a pot of tea and she now poured him a cup. She poured herself a cup as well and they sat without speaking for a few minutes.

They were both startled to hear a key in the front door. Iris had a key for emergencies, but surely, she would have come round to the back door, knowing that Kylie was here. Then the door from the hallway opened.

"Poppy! What are you doing here?" Frank stood up, realising how ludicrous the scene must appear with him wearing a bath robe and with his left arm in a sling.

"Mrs Williams phoned me to tell me you were in hospital," she said. "What on earth have you been doing?" She gave him a quick peck on the cheek, avoiding the injured arm. Frank gave a great sigh.

"I have had to explain all this several times to the police," he said. "Do you really need to know? You didn't need to come all this way, you know."

Kylie poured another cup of tea and all three of them sat comfortably around the table while Frank told the story all over again.

"You could have been killed!" Poppy said.

"I'm not sure he would have stabbed me at all," Frank said, "if I hadn't kicked the stool at him and made him fall forwards."

"In that case, why did he have a knife?"

"It wasn't even his knife," Frank admitted. "He grabbed one of my knives from the block over there. I'm not sure that I shall ever want to use it again after this."

"Where is it?"

"I imagine the police have kept it as evidence."

"The very idea makes me shiver," said Poppy. "You always keep your knives razor-sharp; I know. You were always telling me not to touch them. How much damage has he done?"

"I was lucky," Frank said. "It was a nasty cut, but it missed all the essential bits like arteries and nerves. It'll get better in time."

"Thank God for that!"

"Meanwhile, I've got to get used to washing and dressing with one hand. It's not simple, I've discovered."

"I suppose at least you will get a few weeks more off work."

"No. My job is not very physical these days, especially at this time of year. It's all office work. I still have my right hand, so I can use a pen and my phone. I don't need any more time at home."

"Kylie," Poppy exclaimed, "can you persuade this silly old man he needs to take things easy for a while?"

"I wouldn't dream of it," said Kylie. "I'm going to work extra hard for a few weeks. He has already told me he wants me to do the cooking."

"Well, that is a surprise! It's also quite a compliment, you know."

"I promise you I'll look after him. I owe him a lot."

"What about yourself? You didn't get off exactly scot-free, did you?"

"It's not the first time this has happened to me," Kylie admitted. "I was more scared for the children. When he'd been drinking or on drugs, Gus was very free with his fists. He was always ready to knock me about and he has treated Oliver in the same way. Ollie was terrified, and I could do nothing because I was already lying on the floor, half unconscious. Your father is something of a hero."

"Don't talk rubbish, Kylie," said Frank. "The man made me really angry. He had invaded my home, and this place has always been like a sanctuary, always a pleasant, welcoming place to come back to. And then he terrified two small children, two children I have grown very fond of, as you know. But then he actually knocked you to the ground! When he came towards me, I was absolutely furious. I suppose I was half prepared for it, that's why I had my foot hooked round the stool. Anyway, that was yesterday. It's in the past. Let's try to forget it."

The two women were silent.

"Now you are here," Frank said, looking at Poppy, "you can come upstairs with me to my bedroom and help me into a clean shirt. I can't ask Kylie to do that kind of thing for me."

"Okay," said Poppy, "but what are you going to do when I'm not here?"

"I'm hoping that it will be less painful tomorrow."

Poppy helped him put on a new shirt, drawing the left sleeve carefully over his arm. It was obviously still painful. He would, she said, have to enlist Kylie's help.

"She thinks the world of you," she told him. "Don't be embarrassed. She is far too young to have designs on you." But, she thought, he was still a remarkably fit man for his age. She did up the last button, adjusted his sling, and tidied his hair.

"Apart from your problems with your clothes and your shower," she said, "I think you're going to be okay. I hope you will forgive me, if I dash off first thing in the morning, now I know that you're all right. I'm so glad you have Kylie here."

"Oh well," her father said, "I must be grateful for small mercies. Thank you for coming. I have no idea what Kylie can serve up for dinner."

Iris brought the two children back. She had kept them busy all morning, finding some of the toys and games her own children had used years previously. Emma and Ollie found it all intriguing. Iris explained to them that their mother was busy clearing up after yesterday's mayhem. She fed them macaroni cheese before bringing them back.

Poppy, who left early but who was now less anxious about her father's condition, excused herself and used her laptop to hold a couple of conversations with colleagues.

Somehow, Frank managed to struggle into a large coat by draping it around his shoulders like a 19th-century general on the field of battle. He left the two women to get on with their own tasks and made his way out to the garden. It was cold. Nothing was growing. Deep in the soil bulbs and corms were storing energy in preparation for spring, but the trees had all shed their leaves. Hidden from sight, birds at the bottom of the garden were feeding on berries. Frank stood in the still air, enjoying the peace.

"Does it hurt?" a child's voice, Emma's. She was standing about six feet from him.

"Emma," Frank said, "come here." He crouched to be at her height. When she reached him, he put out his good arm and drew her into an embrace. Ollie was not far behind her. "You, too, Ollie," said Frank, and the boy came close enough for Frank to enclose both of them in his arm.

"Yes," he said into this bundle of youth, vitality, and warmth, "it hurts, but it will get better. As long as you don't bang it or anything."

"You were very brave," Emma said.

"Not really," Frank said, "I want to thank Ollie especially. He was the brave one. He was the one who went running up the stairs with you to get the towel for my arm. I expect you were both absolutely scared stiff. I was."

They both hugged him a little tighter.

"You mustn't think too badly of Gus," Frank said, conscious of the fact that he was talking about their father, "he's not really well, you know."

"I never want to see him again," Ollie said. "He didn't hit me this time. He did last time I saw him. He knocked out one of my teeth."

"Well, he's not going to be around for a very long time," Frank said. "They've locked him up."

"Is he going to get out again?"

"Not for a very long time. You will probably be grown-up by then."

"If he hits Mummy again," Ollie said, "I'll kill him."

"You mustn't talk like that," Frank said.

"Why not?"

"Because it means you would be no better than him."

"Yes, well..."

"I think we should go in out of the cold. I think a mug of hot chocolate would be a good idea. What do you think?"

They separated and made their way back into the warmth of the kitchen where Kylie set about making drinks for everybody.

By the end of the first day at home Frank realised that he was not yet ready to go back to work after all. He was quite frustrated. There was nothing much he could do at home except interrupt Kylie at her work, watch television or listen to the radio. Even reading was difficult with one hand. At this time of the year there was nothing he could do in the garden. The ground was still rock-hard. His arm throbbed for the first week. Kylie, recognising his bad mood, kept out of his way for most of the day. On the third day he tried to teach her how to prepare a complicated menu. She was not familiar with half the ingredients and he founded it very difficult to remain calm. She did her best to humour him, but he never repeated the experiment and was obliged to accept simple, traditional fare. It was enjoyable, but he missed the occasional, more exotic dishes.

Chapter eleven

Despite the trauma of Gus's attack, Kylie remained grateful and not a little surprised that Fank was in no hurry to get her out of the house.

Casual friends and acquaintances may have had their private opinions on the subject, but they kept them largely to themselves. Poppy remained concerned, but said nothing, waiting for her father to do the right thing. Meanwhile she was grateful to Kylie for the care she afforded him, the only exception was Janice.

"I feel partially responsible," she explained apologetically over dinner. Frank was a frequent guest at their house.

"Why on earth should you feel responsible for the wanton acts of a drug addict?" Frank asked in surprise.

"I was the one who introduced you to Kylie in the first place."

"True, and I'm still grateful. She has been a great help and has become a friend. I'm fond of the children, too."

"Yes, but I knew a little about her past and about Gus. I'm the person who got you mixed up in that situation."

"Janice," said Frank, "Kylie has been good for me and she has looked after me very well."

"It was her ex-partner who tried to kill you."

"Well, I'm still inclined to blame the addiction, and I was never convinced he wanted to kill me."

"" The jury thought he did," Janice's husband reminded Frank.

There was a moment's silence, broken only by the sounds of cutlery on the dinner plates.

"The thing is," Janice resumed, not willing to drop the subject, "it could happen again."

Frank was about to argue when she waved a hand to stop him, not thinking how it looked to brandish a knife.

"The thing is," she resumed, "Kylie is a young woman, several years younger than Poppy. One of these days it wouldn't be surprising if she found another young man she fancied, or one who fancied her."

It was a thought that had not entered Frank's head.

"All the time she lives with you," Janice continued, "she has the run of the house. She might invite a boyfriend in all innocence to come in. I'm not even suggesting he might attack you with or without a knife, but he could wander anywhere and pick up anything he fancied. Neither you nor Kylie need know about it."

"Do you think that's likely?"

"Likely or not, it's possible, surely."

Frank frowned at the unpleasant thought. Janice took the plates to the kitchen.

"We have always agreed it was only a temporary arrangement," Frank said.

"Do you realise you've made it harder for Kylie to get onto any community housing list? Not only will she be less than eager to leave such a comfortable home, any of the agencies like the Council housing list will see that her case is not especially urgent now."

Frank walked home feeling unsettled.

In June an official-looking letter arrived, addressed to Miss Poppy Whitaker. Frank was puzzled. He phoned Poppy to tell her but, before he could break the news, she was talking excitedly to him.

"I'm pregnant!"

"Oh, congratulations! I am very pleased for you. You must be delighted!"

"We are, we are. We now have to think about furnishing a nursery and buying all the stuff you need for a baby. It is really exciting news. It was only confirmed this morning."

"Absolutely wonderful! Now take good care of yourself, won't you?"

"Yes, of course I will. There is a very good antenatal clinic and I shall be a model patient."

In all the excitement Frank almost full got why he had called in the first instance. When he remembered, it did not seem so important. He would drive up to see them at the weekend, he said, and bring the letter with him.

Poppy was still very excited by her pregnancy and took the letter from Frank almost casually, chattering on. Finally, realising she was holding it in her hand, she found a paper knife and slit open the envelope. A sheet of paper was headed by the name of a legal firm, a name which was unfamiliar to her and to her father. Puzzled, she read the letter. The writer explained that he and his firm were retained by the owners of the residential home where her great aunt had lived. Aunt Betty, it informed her, had died intestate, several weeks earlier. It was usual in such circumstances for the estate to go to the Exchequer, unless and next of kin could be traced. The Matron of the residential home recalled the visit made by Frank Whitaker and his daughter. They had been unable to trace any other relatives and Mr Whitaker would normally inherit whatever estate there was. However, Mrs Kristinin had drawn up a will which they had found when clearing her room. The will, though signed and dated, had not been witnessed and was therefore invalid. It expressed a preference for all her belongings to go to her great-niece, Poppy Whitaker. She was therefore asked to arrange a visit to the Home and to discuss the matter with her father. A copy of the same letter would be sent to Mr Frank Whitaker. They would both need to bring proof of identity. It would be most convenient if they could both come to the Home so that the matter could be satisfactorily resolved.

Frank had not received his copy.

"I shouldn't think she left much," Frank said. "That place must be very expensive place to stay. Whatever she had, it will have gone on the Home."

"I can't imagine why she would want to leave it to me, anyway," Poppy said.

"She must have taken a fancy to you."

"Maybe. I suppose we could all drive down there. Martin has never been anywhere near Oakmere. We could treat it as a kind of day out."

"Whatever you say."

A phone call provoked an apology and confirmation of the unusual arrangement.

After several further letters and phone calls, a date was arranged. Frank could arrange his own time, but Martin and Poppy had to negotiate days off work. Frank stayed the night with them and the following morning Martin drove his comfortable, family saloon to Oakmere. Conversation tended to centre on preparations for the new arrival rather than on the unexpected and mildly intriguing legacy. They arrived in a carefree mood. They were ten minutes early. The Matron had set out four chairs in a room where she said they would not be disturbed. She brought in a tray of coffee and biscuits for them and left. The solicitor arrived dead on time. Mr Chester was a genial man in his forties. He introduced himself and expressed mild surprise to be faced by three visitors.

"I assume," he said, "that you are Miss Poppy Whittaker and that you, sir, are her father, Frank Whitaker."

"Yes, that's right," Frank said.

"My name is Martin Balmain, Poppy's husband."

"Oh! I was not aware that you had married. That must have been since you came here to visit your aunt."

"Yes, a little after then."

"Well, my congratulations to you both. I'm afraid I must ask for confirmation of your identities, at least yours, Mrs Balmain, and yours Mr Whitaker. I don't know if you have brought the necessary documents with you?"

"We sort of expected this," Poppy said. "I have brought my birth certificate and our marriage certificate."

"Splendid! If I may just look at them for a moment…"

Poppy took an envelope out of her handbag and gave it to him. He looked quickly at the two documents.

"Good," he said, "so we can get on with the business in hand. As I believe I told you in my letter, your aunt left what she thought was a will, but it was not witnessed and so not legal. Normally, if one of the residents of this home passes away, and they leave no will to indicate what to do with the estate, we are called in to look for the next of kin. If we can find nobody, the estate belongs to the Crown. Any belongings may be sold and the monies so realised are held for some time come available if relatives come forward to claim them. To speed up such a process in the first instance we have been called in to identify any legal heirs. I am afraid we charge a fee for the service which comes from the value of the estate."

"I shouldn't imagine there will be very much to pay you with," Frank observed.

"I think you might be pleasantly surprised," said Mr Chester. "Some years ago, when your aunt's husband died, Mrs Kristinin inherited a shop and the house in which they lived. She sold both properties. Also, I believe unknown to her, Mr Kristinin held a portfolio of shares. The revenue from those shares and the capital which she also invested has been enough to pay for her residence in this home. She left a very few possessions, in fact, apart from her clothes which we have already disposed of, everything from her room is stowed in the cabin trunk which you can see over there." He turned in his chair and pointed to a round-topped cabin trunk next to the wall. "It contains personal items, such as her dressing table set of brushes and bottles, a gold necklace, a rather nice clock, and a radio. There were a number of paperbacks which we have disposed of, but we held onto a dozen hardback books. There was also a bundle of papers relating to the sale of the two properties I've mentioned and what appears to be a set of accounts dating back many years. Tied up with the account books there is also a small, steel box which is locked. A label on the top in very neat, but small handwriting reads 'unredeemed'. Your aunt appears to have been fairly parsimonious with her money, but she has left approximately £60,000 in her bank account, as well as the shares. The shares are probably worth about £90,000 in today's market. It would appear that legally you, Mr Whitaker, are the first in line to inherit. Our fee is 15% of the estate. Bearing in mind the un-witnessed will, you may wish to pass on some or all of this money to your daughter."

Frank, Poppy, and Martin stared at the man in disbelief.

"You may, of course, challenge all this. I promise you that we have done everything we can and that there is no one else we can find who might have any claim on the estate. If you agree to our terms, that is, the 15% fee, I can go ahead and make all the necessary arrangements for the transfer of everything in the estate."

Frank and Poppy were both still stunned. After a moment Frank shook his head, unable to believe what he had been told. "She would have hated me to inherit this," he said. "When I was a young boy, she showed me nothing but coldness. She resented my very existence and she virtually told me that when we came here the last time."

"Don't you think," Martin asked, "there is some kind of justice in your inheriting all this? There is a sort of irony about it, don't you think?"

Frank looked at him, not able to take it in.

"There's just one other thing," said the solicitor, "the trunk over there, it's in the way, the Matron says. I see no reason why you shouldn't take that away with you. It is very heavy. But I really need to know if you accept the terms."

"Yes." He would pass it all on to Poppy, Frank was thinking. She in turn could ensure that the baby, when it was born, would have a head start.

Mr Chester had brought copies of the agreement with him. He now spread them in front of Frank and Poppy and explained the terms. An hour later the matron appeared, remove the old tray, and came back with a new one. The documents were signed and dated.

Frank kept one copy, the other was removed by a smiling Mr Chester.

"Well," he said, "it will take a week or two to sort all this out. I'll be in touch. It has been a pleasure to meet you all and I hope you will enjoy the money eventually." He shook hands with the three of them, knocked on the door through which the Matron had disappeared, thanked her for the tea when she reappeared, shook her hand, and said he would be in touch with her, then he left.

"Are you going to take that wretched trunk away?" the Matron asked.

"Yes, we'll take it," Frank said.

"Just this once you can bring your car round to the front door. That trunk is very heavy."

Poppy brought the car round and positioned it as close to the front door as she could. The cabin trunk was exceedingly heavy. Frank and Martin each took one of the handles but they could only carry it for all of 5 yards at a time. They had to stop halfway across the hall, and again on the steps outside the door. The final effort, lifting it into the boot of the car required all their strength and it was noticeable that the vehicle sank several inches at the back.

They drove back to Poppy's house. At her suggestion, they unlocked the cabin trunk and removed the heavy books and carried them indoors separately to lighten the rest. Even so, it was still as much as Martin and Frank could do to carry the rest of it into the living room and put it down in the middle of the floor. It would, they thought, be a dull task to empty the rest of the contents. They were two or three bundles of legal-looking papers, tied up with pink ribbon. These they piled up to be looked at later. They would probably end up in the recycling. The account books had not been opened for years. Frank opened one and realised it was a day book from the pawnbrokers. In his uncle Vladimir's meticulous writing was a record of the daily transactions. Each piece of jewellery or other precious belonging was recorded with an identifiable number. Alongside worthy names and addresses of those who have left their belongings as pledges. One: column showed the amount of money handed over for each item. The dates went) to the 1940s but even so Frank was shocked by the tiny amounts of money given out. The people of Oakmere, or many of them, must have suffered hardship. Many of the entries were for gold rings, presumably their wedding rings, for which they were loaned about 10 shillings. There were one or two curious items which had been pledged, a pair of skis, a silver cup, even a rocking horse. Here and there items of jewellery were listed. Many of the pledges were redeemed. The amount of money returned was shown together with the date. For full there were, however, some items which had clearly never been claimed and, since the book had been in use for six years, there had to be more than one or two unaccounted for. When he reached that conclusion, he suddenly realised the significance of the word written on top of the small, metal box.' 'Unredeemed' must surely be deferred to the items which had never been claimed. The box was locked but it held no sentimental significance for Frank or Poppy. Martin found his toolbox which contained basic tools, hardly ever used. He found a chisel and a hammer and took the box outside. Frank watched with amusement as his son-in-law set to work on the hasp. It proved quite difficult, but at last the lid was released. Carefully they took the now badly battered box back into the kitchen and put it on the table. The three of them gathered round, feeling like children about to discover hidden treasure.

"This is like a pirates' treasure chest," said Poppy. "I'm expecting it to be full of jewels and gold coins." The others laughed as she lifted the lid.

Inside, the first thing they noticed was scores of small paper labels, each one seemingly attached to 1 of the objects. There were six or seven rings, four of them gold. Each ring had its own label with a number and Frank realised that the numbers must correspond to the entries in the book. He checked two of them and found that was the case. There were a number of brooches, one or two necklaces, three small pendants. They spread the contents across the table. They made a pitiful collection and represented something quite moving: each of these objects had been handed over for a few shillings because the owner was desperate. None of them appeared to be very valuable except for a yellowing envelope which contained four gold sovereigns. Frank wondered how the owner could have left them. Poppy pushing the brooches and jewellery around as she looked at them in turn, sorted out half a dozen brooches and necklaces which looked especially pretty. There were two brooches in particular, one in the shape of a dragonfly, another in an abstract design, both seem to be very well made, quality pieces of costume jewellery. She picked up the abstract design and handed it to Martin and asked him what he thought of it. He looked at it, turned it over to look at the back, and exclaimed, "It's hallmarked!" Frank checked the number against the entry in the book, the item was only listed as 'brooch' and valued at two pounds.

"" Maybe this really is a kind of treasure trove," he said. "Have another look at the really nice pieces." Of all the pieces in the box – they counted fifty-three altogether – there were six which seemed especially good.

"Just for fun," Poppy said, "I think I'm going to take these along to the local jeweller to get them valued."

Frank drove home, still not believing that he was the heir to a considerable sum of money. Morally, he thought, it belonged to his daughter. Legally it belonged to him.

Poppy was reluctant to accept the money. That was no surprise to Frank, though it was annoying. The argument took several weeks to resolve. It took some time, too, to complete all the legal requirements with Mr Chester. Poppy, meanwhile, had taken two of the brooches to the local jeweller who said he was not competent to value them. The stones were real, he said, not paste. The legacy was proving to be far more valuable than any of them had expected. The gold sovereigns, which had a face value of twenty shillings each would clearly be worth more than that, but they were shocked to find they were worth £160 each. Poppy then took the two brooches to an auction house to be valued. One, she was told, would probably fetch between two and £3000 at auction, the other about £2000. She wasted no time in phoning her father with the news.

Frank was curiously disturbed by all this. Whenever he thought of Aunt Betty, it was with distaste. She had never showed him any affection. She had even proposed leaving everything she had to his daughter rather than to Frank himself. He was very uncertain how he felt about accepting any of her wealth. Poppy was insistent that he should accept it all. They finally arrived at a compromise: take the contents of the cabin trunk and he would inherit the rest. Privately, Frank intended to leave everything to Poppy in his will. And so, the matter was settled. Poppy was delighted. The money would furnish the new nursery with much of the necessary material needed for a new baby. She saw the whole thing as a kind of metaphor of death and rebirth.

They were still wrangling over the allocation of these newly acquired riches, when Frank and Kylie were required to attend court as witnesses for the first appearance of Gus. He had been charged with more than one crime including assault, demanding money with menaces, causing actual bodily harm with a sharp knife. After the magistrates' court, he was remanded in custody for trial at the County Court. Given his existing record and the fact that he was a known heroin addict, he was likely to be locked away for a long time yet.

"I hope his sentence is long enough," Frank said as they drove home," for him to undergo a proper course of treatment. There must be some good in the man. After all, Kylie, you chose him to father your children."

"You are always far too understanding," she said. "I can never forgive him. He not only knocked me about, remember, Ollie received the same kind of treatment on more than one occasion. And as for choosing him as a partner, I was very young. I bitterly regret it. I don't care if he never comes out of prison."

Frank said no more. The two children might be destined to grow up without a father. It had happened to him. The circumstances had been quite different, and, thank God, people did not heap shame on single mothers, even unmarried mothers these days. He was far too old to take on the role of a substitute father, but he was quite happy for the children to look on n him as they would on a grandfather. He was quite fond of all of them.

For the time being he had forgotten the conversation with Janice, reminding him of the long-term aim of finding a more permanent home for Kylie and her children.

Chapter twelve

Kylie was surprised one morning when Frank did not leave for work. Instead, he appeared in the kitchen where she had already given her children breakfast. He was wearing a suit and seemed reluctant to chat. He made himself coffee and toast. Not knowing what was wrong, she simply kept silent, cleared away the dishes and then slipped out of the kitchen. Frank walked down the garden and returned with a quantity of flowers. Some of them he arranged in a vase on the kitchen table. The rest he tied into a crude bouquet which he carried out to the car together with another vase before driving off.

He drove to the school. Janice, seeing him arrive, left her class for a moment, asking a young colleague to keep an eye on them, and hurried out to meet him.

"Frank," she said, "I am so sorry. I had forgotten."

This was the day when, one year ago, Louise had lost her battle and died. Frank retrieved the flowers and the vase and the two of them walked down the grounds to the gardens Frank and his wife had worked so hard to create. Beyond the flourishing vegetable patch, the grass, soggy after so much rain, stretched to the circular seat which surrounded the tree planted in Louise's memory. Frank placed the flowers at the foot of the tree, a small and inadequate tribute, and then he stood for a while in thought. Janice stood with him but said nothing. At length Frank turned away and the two of them walked back to the car.

"You have had a hard year," Janice said, closing the car door behind him. "But you have achieved a number of find things, not least taking in Kylie and her children. Louise would be proud of you."

Frank merely nodded, not trusting himself to speak. That he drove home.

Kylie, not knowing the reason for Frank's unusual behaviour, thought it best to keep out of his way. It was a fine day after all the rain. Frank took a warm coat from the peg in the hallway, picked up an old anorak, and walked to the end of his precious garden. There, out of sight, he draped the anorak over the damp wood and sat down to gaze at the garden he and Louise had made. He could remember every detail, the planting of every, cherished shrub. Conversations, discussions, came back and he heard her voice as clear as if she were sitting with him. He forgot about time until Kylie, getting worried, tracked him down, still huddled in his coat, staring into space.

"Are you all right?" she asked.

Frank lifted his head and looked at her. His expression was one of pure anguish. The recall to a real world of bare trees and muddy grass was like being plunged into cold water. To Kylie's dismay, instead of replying, his face crumpled and he buried his head in his hands. She moved swiftly and instinctively to sit beside him and put her arms round him, pulling him to her as she would with one of her children. He did not resist but cried as though, indeed, he was a small child. It was an outpouring of grief which was more intense than anything Kylie had seen before. The weeping went on for several minutes, then Frank pulled away, his gaze averted, ashamed.

"It's getting chilly," she said. "Let's get you inside."

He stood up and allowed her to take his arm and guide him over the wet ground to the kitchen door. He moved like an old man, head down, shoulders slumped.

He sat down heavily, not taking off his coat.

"Don't move," Kylie ordered. "I'll heat up some soup."

"Kylie," Frank said, as she opened a container of soup which he had made himself and which she would heat in the microwave, "I'm sorry…"

"There's no need to explain," she said. "Just take off that coat. You'll feel better when you've had something to eat."

He removed his coat. She served the soup, together with a thick slice of bread. He ate with growing appetite, still avoiding her eyes.

"If you've finished," she said, "why don't you have a bath to warm up?"

It was a good excuse for him to escape. His face felt puffy. He felt embarrassed, the memory of her motherly, comforting embrace still vivid. He nodded and left the kitchen to the sanctuary of his room. There was no bath, but he stood for a while in the hot shower before he put away the suit he had been wearing, and dressed in clean, casual clothes. The suit would need cleaning.

It was as though the shower or more probably the tears had washed away his emotions. He felt numb. He was also exhausted.

Once again, he tried to apologise. Once again Kylie stopped him. "Don't say anything," she said. "I should be apologising to you for intruding. You're looking better. I'll make a pot of tea."

"Louise died a year ago today," he said.

"Oh! Now I understand."

"Thank you for looking after me," he said.

"Will you be OK if I go and get the kids? I'll make sure to keep them out of your way."

"Don't do that. Bring them in here. There's no need for any of this to affect them and I like to have them around."

He drank the tea she had prepared. The overwhelming and sudden experience of grief had been cathartic. It left him tired but the persistent, nagging unhappiness which had dogged him for so long had given way to calm. It was as though he had kissed Louise a last farewell.

Poppy phoned and was surprised and reassured to discover her father able to hold a conversation in such a calm state of mind. He told her how he had taken cut flowers to the 'memorial tree'. He turned the conversation to ask how she was, and how plans were progressing. When she rang off, she turned to her husband and remarked, "He actually sounds better. I thought he would be really low today, but he sounded brighter. He seems ready to let go of the past and concentrate on the future.".

"Can I borrow one of your cookbooks?" asked Kylie.

"No. I never lend tools or equipment. What do you want it for?"

Kylie looked crestfallen.

"I want to bake a special birthday cake," she explained. "The children's birthdays are only a week apart. I was hoping to do something special for them this year."

"When is this?

Kylie told him. The birthdays were two weeks ahead.

"Let me bake them a cake," he said.

"That's very kind of you, but I really want to do this myself."

"Compromise," said Frank," 'Ill cook it and you ice it."

Kylie was busy over the next few days. Icing was altogether more difficult than she had thought. In the end she decided to smother the cake in chocolate icing and have two clusters of candles, nine on one side, seven on the other.

It was the first time she had been able to buy decent presents. She explained the birthday tea would be for both of them. She asked, half-heartedly, if either of them wanted to invite friends from school but, to her surprise and relief, both said no. Emma's birthday came first, so Kylie gave her a card and a small present and told her she would provide another present on the joint birthday. It went according to plan. Frank was invited to share the fun for a while. He gave each of them a small savings book with five pounds in it. Mysteriously, he said he would 'do something for them on Ollie's real birthday".

Ollie's birthday fell on a Saturday. Having warned Kylie the previous day, Frank ushered her with the children into his car, which he had cleaned specially.

"Where are we going?" Emma asked.

"A mystery ride," said Frank. "Even your mother doesn't know."

After an hour the children were beginning to get restless and impatient.

"Are we nearly there yet?" Ollie asked.

"Two more minutes."

He turned left into a wide gateway. A large, painted arch read, 'Jingleside Fun Park.' Frank led the way through the entrance. Coloured lights flashed everywhere and a noisy roller-coaster roared above them Kylie, Ollie and Emma stared, spellbound, as Frank paid at the entrance. There were crowds of people milling about, all seemingly happy, many of them eating hotdogs, ice-creams, bags of strange-smelling foodstuffs. Frank manoeuvred them into a nearby café area, bought them drinks, opened the brightly coloured map he had been given, and asked what rides they fancied. The roller-coaster, unfortunately, was only open for bigger people, but there were plenty of other attractions, some they could all share, like the water ride. After hours spent walking from one ride to another to be shaken and spun and thrown about, even Frank, who considered himself fit, began to grow weary. For the fifth time Kylie took Emma on the large carrousel while Frank and Ollie were hurled round in the sky.

"Time for a drink," said Frank, as the four of them joined up again. Then, as they sat with drinks at a table, "One more ride, then we'll have to be getting home."

Emma and her brother wanted different rides so they split up again for the last time. This time the grown-ups watched as the two children climbed on the rides. Frank looked at Kylie surreptitiously. She looked curiously sad at moments.

"Are you feeling unwell?" he asked her as quietly as the loud music allowed.

"No," she replied, startled by the question, "What makes you ask?"

"You look tired, or has all this given you a headache?"

She did not reply at first, but waved to her daughter as she passed. "Can I say something?" she said. "But please don't be offended."

He frowned, not knowing what was coming.

"All this is too much," she said. "You keep doing so much for us it makes me feel inadequate. This outing is – well- unbelievable. It must have cost you a small fortune."

"Oh, my goodness!" Frank looked back at her and for the first time understood her embarrassment. "Kylie, I'm doing this for Ollie and Emma. They've brought so much pleasure into my life when I most needed it. No one ever did this sort of thing for me when I was small. As for the cost, well, it's probably the price of a couple of sovereigns."

Kylie could think of nothing to reply, though she was puzzled by the way he spoke of sovereigns. They stood side by side as the roundabout began to slow down. Frank took her by the shoulders and added, "Thank you for letting me share your children today." Then he gave her a sudden, short hug before striding off to collect Ollie.

Emma fell asleep in her mother's arms on the back seat. Ollie chattered excitedly for a while until finally he became drowsy. When they arrived home at last Kylie took them indoors, saying, "Thank you so much. I'd better get these two to bed."

The following morning, Sunday, Frank made himself a simple breakfast and wandered into the garden a pair of secateurs in his hand. The air was cool and fresh and down amongst the trees almost the only sound was that of church bells. It was a sharp contrast with the noise of the theme park. Frank felt relaxed and rested. The children came running down after a while. They threw themselves at him, then Ollie pulled away and thanked Frank for their birthday present. They chattered for a short time, recalling some of the adventures, but then said they had to go back indoors. Frank watched the two small figures disappear among the apple trees and turned back to his pruning.

But something had changed. There was a new element of constraint between Kylie and himself. His affection for the children remained as strong as ever but he realised his generosity was inappropriate in Kylie's eyes. She had been embarrassed.

It was Kylie who brought the subject into the open.

"Can I say something?" she asked, two days after the birthday treat.

"Say something?"

"The situation is sort of awkward."

"I thought there was something wrong."

"Yes."

"What has happened?"

"It's hard to explain," said Kylie. She sat down at the kitchen table. "It's your treat. It's made me think."

"What are you talking about?"

"I know taking the children out for the day was very kind."

"They enjoyed it, didn't they?"

"They loved it, of course they did. The thing is, it was something I could never have done for them"

"That's why I thought of it."

Kylie was finding it difficult to explain. "But that's just it," she said. "I feel a bit like – well, as if you've taken over my children. It's not as though they're your grandchildren, and I'm not your daughter."

"Oh!" Frank was genuinely surprised. "I'm very fond of your children," he said, "but I never thought in that way."

"You have been so kind to us," Kylie repeated. "That's what makes it so hard for me to talk about it like this."

"The last thing I want is to upset you," Frank said. "I thought we were getting along pretty well. You've been very good, looking after me. And sharing this big house suits me."

"Have you ever thought how other people might see it?"

"What do you mean?"

"Well, you invite me into your lovely home and let me share it with you. Tongues will wag."

Frank looked at he in shock. "Are you suggesting...?" he began. "But you're even younger than my own daughter. Poppy is thirty-one. How could people...?"

"I know that," said Kylie, but you have to admit it could be – well, misinterpreted. We've seen one another at times of stress and I admit – well, the way you treat me and the children, it sort of makes me feel sort of fond of you. I think you feel the same."

Frank was at a loss for a while.

"Of course, I've grown fond of you," he said. "There's nothing wrong with that. And I know you aren't my daughter. Does it matter what other people think?"

"Yes! I don't want to be seen as someone taking advantage of a man who has lost his wife, especially when the man is old enough to be my father."

Frank frowned at her but did not reply for some time. Kylie looked anxious, as though wondering if she had said too much.

"So," Frank said at last, "what do you want to do?"

"I don't know. I suppose I want to remain good friends, but without the extravagant gestures. This will sound silly, but, if I am your housekeeper, I should wear a kind of uniform, and we shouldn't socialise."

"Socialise?"

"Things like sharing a pot of tea and gossiping."

"Is that what you really want?"

She nodded. "I think it would be best, and the children would see the situation better, you, the employer, me, the employee."

"OK. I'm sorry if I've embarrassed you."

"Friends?"

"Friends."

A phone call from Martin helped his emotional readjustment. Poppy had given birth.

"It's a boy!" Martin's excitement on the phone made him sound almost boyish. "Seven pounds and one ounce and perfect. Poppy is fine, very tired. They want to keep in for two nights, then I can take them both home. If you can bear to wait that long, you can come and meet your grandson then."

Frank thanked him and later he spoke to his daughter, congratulating her. He would have driven up the same day, but it made sense to give Poppy a day or two to recover. He was impatient to see the baby. Three days later he drove to his daughter's house with a large bunch of flowers, a splendid, silver christening mug, and a broad smile on his face. He rang the front doorbell. It was opened by Martin's mother, Esther. This was something Frank had not been entirely ready for. Esther, he learned, had arrived at the same time as the baby, keen to help Poppy. Frank smiled at her and made his way to the small sitting room where his daughter sat with the baby in her arms. He kissed them both and Esther took the flowers to put them in water. Roger, Martin's father, was sitting in an armchair. The two men greeted each other. The room already felt a little crowded.

Anticipating the birth of his first grandchild, Frank had somehow ignored any thought of Esther and Roger. He had met them several times. They were a little older than he was and Roger had been retired for several years. Roger was not a great talker. The three of them had been standing in the newly planted garden some weeks previously when Esther admitted she found gardening boring. Her hobby and interest was bridge, which she played regularly several afternoons every week. She asked Frank what his hobby was, a question he found difficult to answer, because his work was also his hobby. He had asked the monosyllabic Roger how he spent his spare time now he was retired.

"Golf," he said.

"Golf?"

"Wednesdays and Saturday's. Eighteen holes."

"And the Nineteenth," Esther added with a mildly disapproving tone.

The only thing they had in common with Frank, it would seem, was the couple that were establishing their home together. With the arrival of the baby, they all shared something far more precious and identifiable. Frank was not altogether prepared for it. He added assumed quite unreasonably that he was going to acquire a grandson with whom he would share a close relationship of the kind he had always shared with his daughter. Finding Esther and Roger at the house, seemingly at home and busy with housework and, in Esther's case, the physical care of the child, Frank was obliged to accept that he was no more entitled to a unique relationship than they were. It came as a shock.

"What about a name? "He asked Poppy. ""

"We've decided on Oscar," she said.

"Oh!" Frank could think of nothing to add.

"We also agreed," Martin added, "to avoid arguments, to give him middle names from both grandparents. He's going to be Oscar Roger Frank Balmain."

"Right," said Frank weakly.

As he drove home later, he was remembering the day, just a few months ago, which he and Poppy had spent together, the carefree, childish exhilaration of paddling in the sea, hand in hand. It would never happen again. Life seemed to be changing inexorably and he had no way of stopping it. He let himself in by the front door. It smelt of furniture polish. Kylie was an excellent housekeeper but her behaviour towards him had undoubtedly changed. She was present but not inclined to chatter. It was like losing a friend.

He phoned his daughter the following day for no reason other than the need to hear her voice.

"Daddy," she said, "have you given up your quest to trace your father?"

"I don't think there's anything else I can do. I have hit the buffers, as they say."

"I was talking to Martin's mum," she said. "She's into family history."

"I thought she played bridge."

"She does, but she's also interested in family history. She is joined some kind of online thing."

"I haven't tried that."

"Well, I don't know if you know about this, but you can now send off a DNA sample and they use it to trace your ancestry."

"Tell me more."

"I don't know a lot, but I think it sounds quite exciting. Apparently, there are now millions of people whose genetic profiles – is the word 'genomes'? –are recorded round the world. They take your sample of DNA and try to match it."

"Sounds a bit hit and miss. I imagine it would depend on some distant relative having recorded his DNA already."

"I told you; I don't know how it works. It might be worth a look though."

The conversation with Poppy reawakened his interest. He had given up all hope of finding out more about his father, but it had left him feeling quite frustrated. He began looking into online family history. He noted that the writers of this complicated program, when referring to the DNA research, recommended that it should be combined with documentary research. But Frank had already done a great deal of that, visiting libraries, referring to newspapers, looking up birth and death certificates. He decided to go ahead. It was not expensive. It seemed unlikely that he would discover the full truth, but he had plenty of time. He began by establishing a family tree on his mother's side. It took him back to the village of Larch and his grandparents. But it was not what he was looking for. The DNA sample took some time to produce results, but, when they came, they took him by surprise.

It was possible, he discovered, to use his DNA to trace the male line. In his case it showed that he was strongly connected to people who lived in Canada. The evidence was vague, but showed traces of both Scandinavian and Cree ancestry. It proved impossible to narrow it down. It seemed likely that his father had been a Canadian soldier on his way to the Normandy landings. Whether he survived would be difficult to discover. As time passed, Frank's eagerness to discover the facts diminished. He was under pressure ay work and could pay only brief visits to Oakmere. His life had begun to resume some kind of normality now but it was not a very entertaining routine. With a new kind of austerity imposed, his work was less attractive. At times he felt he was having to drive his men instead of lead them.

Chapter thirteen

His appearance at the Thursday night gathering, unannounced, was welcomed with a loud and confused babble of "Frank!" "" It's the missionary!". "Welcome back!" Frank smiled and raised a hand in recognition. "No daughter this time?" someone asked as he sat down. He explained that Poppy was now married and had a son.

"It's a long way to come to wet the baby's head," a voice called.

"A toast!" said another man, "To mother and baby!" Glasses were raised and Frank smiled broadly, glad to be back in such company.

There was a newcomer in the group. Doc explained the use of the word 'mission' then asked Frank if it had been accomplished.

"Not completely," he said. Steve did not comment. Frank assumed he felt constrained by his professional part in finding Aunt Betty. Frank was ready to talk about that, however. The men listened attentively to the story of his visit to his late aunt. He said nothing about the cabin trunk and its contents. The conversation moved on, became more light-hearted. When Jeremy called, "Time, gentlemen, please," Frank was surprised how quickly the evening had gone. It felt as though he had come home.

He returned to the perusal of local newspapers, searching for items about Canadian troops in the area at the time of his mother's rape – he remained convinced there had been a rape. Reports in the press were scanty. It seemed likely that editors were cautious about printing information about troop movements.

He felt frustrated again, but his researches were interrupted by a phone call from Janice.

"I'm sorry to disturb you on your travels," she said, ,,,,,,,,,but this needs a decision quickly."

"Decision? About what?"

"It's very complicated," Janice said. "I think I may have a solution to the housing problem for Kylie and her children, but I don't want to interfere and talk to Kylie before speaking to you. I take it the present arrangement is still temporary?"

"Well, yes," said Frank. "The plan has always been that she would continue looking for a suitable place of her own."

"This is far too complicated to explain on the phone," said Janice. "How long will you be away?"

"If it's urgent and will solve Kylie's problems, I can come back tomorrow."

"That would be wonderful," Janice said, "but I feel guilty about interfering with your plans."

"I'll be with you tomorrow afternoon."

He was not getting much further with his researches, and Janice's strange sense of urgency tipped the balance. He wondered what this curious scheme was all about.

"Oh, Frank, thank you so much for coming!" Janice stepped aside to allow him to walk into her familiar, comfortable sitting room. "Can I get you a cup of tea?"

Frank refused the offer.

"Friends of mine," Janice began, "are Philip and Maria Vallings. Philip is a molecular biologist. He works at the Polytechnic. He has been offered a research post in Leicester and he has to decide within the next two weeks. He is very keen to accept, but there is a big snag."

Frank listened, wondering how this could relate to himself and to Kylie.

"Philip and Maria live in a three-bedroomed house on Pittsburg Street. They have two boys in their early teens. They also have a granny flat attached to the house where Maria's mother lives. Mrs Delgado – you'd never know she was Spanish, by the way – is absolutely adamant she won't move. She would be perfectly happy for the rest of the family to move, but she refuses to go with them,"

"And they want to sell the house," Frank concluded.

"Not necessarily, no. There is a perfectly good house available for them in Leicester."

"So, it's a matter of persuading this Mrs Degado to change her mind?"

"She won't. The trouble is she seems fit and able and very active. She has lots of friends and gets out and about."

"Sounds very independent."

"She is. The trouble is that she has a heart condition and really needs someone to look out for her. The granny flat has been ideal."

"Where is all this leading?" asked Frank. "I hope you aren't going to suggest she moves in with me."

Janice laughed. "No, of course not. I know Maria and her mother and Philip. I know their children, too. As I understand it, this job that Philip has been offered could be a huge opportunity for him., a real life-changer"

"Janice, you seem to spend half your life organising things for others. What's your plan for this family?"

Janice sat back in her chair and took a deep breath. "It may not work," she said, "but I think it could. What if Kylie and her children moved into the house? I believe the Vallings would be happy to let her stay there and keep an eye on Maria's mum. She would have a house of her own to all intents and purposes and there would be someone to look out for Victoria."

"What if she doesn't like Kylie, or vice versa?"

"Well, of course that is the biggest hurdle, but, as I said, Victoria is a very sociable, independent lady, far more active than you would expect.

She's a few years older than you, by the way, and sharp as a needle."

Frank stared at her, shaking his head slowly with a mixture of wonder and admiration.

"Time is of the essence," Janice said. "Do you think we could persuade Kylie to meet Philip, Maria and especially Victoria?"

"Surely you need to find out if the Vallings and Mrs Delgado are prepared to go along with this first."

"I'm pretty sure of that. I have to admit I've suggested the idea in principle. The obvious drawback was, as you say., making sure any new tenant would get on with Victoria. Knowing Kylie, I'm sure they would get along well. Victoria likes children, by the way, and Ollie and Emma would soon charm her. They've worked their charm on you after all."

Frank found Kylie busy in the kitchen. She had not expected him to return from Oakmere.

"I had to come back early," was all he said by way of explanation. He watched while Kylie gave the children a drink and a snack. She made him a pot of tea.

"Please join me," Frank said. "I have something important to ask you. Let the children play in the garden for a bit. We can keep an eye on them from here."

Kylie, mystified, did as he asked. She looked nervous. Frank did not know how to explain other than by mentioning Janice. He presented the plan as coming from Janice. Kylie listened and was astonished.

"Do you want to get rid of us?" she asked.

"It's not like that," Frank said. "I thought we had agreed this arrangement was temporary until you could find somewhere else."

"How would it work?" Kylie asked. "Would they want a deposit? What about rent?"

"I can't answer any of these questions," Frank said. "It all depends on whether you get on with the Vallings family and especially Mrs Delgado."

"And how ill is she? I'm not a trained nurse."

"I don't know much more. I'm told she is very active with lots of friends and very independent.

She wouldn't live with you. The entire house would be yours and the children's'. It's worth looking into, anyway."

Kylie was not entirely convinced but agreed to accompany Frank the following afternoon to the house in Pittsburg Street. The children would be in school. Janet and Philip took the afternoon off and at 2 pm Frank rang the doorbell of the Vallings' house. Kyle stood slightly behind him, looking very nervous.

A dark-haired woman opened the door. She greeted them both and led the way into a sitting room and introduced her husband Philip, a good-looking man of about forty. Janice smiled encouragingly and said hello. On a straight-backed chair sat the lady whom Frank and Kylie presumed to be Victoria. Her hair was black. Her eyes were expertly made up with eye-shadow and mascara and her lipstick was bright. However she dealt with her skin, it appeared to be without blemishes or wrinkles. Even her neck showed no sign of ageing. She could, thought the astonished Frank, be a thirty-year old flamenco dancer. She looked at the newcomers from dark, curious eyes.

"Welcome," she said, looking at Kylie. "This is your father, no?"

"No, Mr Whitaker is my employer."

"Your employer? And you live with him?"

"No, not like that," Kylie corrected her hurriedly. "Mr Whitaker lets me stay in his house with my children."

"Ah!" said Victoria with the suspicion of a wink, "a very convenient arrangement. So, why do you want to escape?"

"Mama!" Maria interrupted, "don't be so naughty." She turned to Kylie, "I'm sorry," she said, "my mother has a warped sense of humour at times. She knows all about your present arrangements." She turned back to Victoria, "I hope Kylie will forgive your bad manners. Are you deliberately trying to put her off?"

But Kylie was smiling. "It's all right, "she said. "I didn't take it seriously. And it's good to have a sense of humour. Sometimes older people seem to lose theirs."

Oh dear, thought Frank, this was not going well, but to everyone's surprise Victoria threw back her elegantly coiffured head and laughed. "I like you, young lady," she said and the others relaxed visibly.

"Maria," Victoria said, "why have you not offered our visitors a cup of tea?"

Maria left the door open as she went to the kitchen to do as her mother commanded. Philip was busy explaining what he and Maria were looking for, since Victoria refused to move.

"Why should I leave all my friends to follow you and Maria to Leicester? I can look after myself. I want you to go. You want to go and everything is set up. You are just trying to use me as an excuse. Go!"

"Mama," said Philip, "that's not true. You are right about looking after yourself, but you know what the doctors say."

"Doctors? They don't know everything. I could drop dead in ten years' time and you could have thrown away the chance of a lifetime for nothing. You have to seize opportunities when they arise. But I am staying here with my dancing and my bridge. Do they even have Flamenco dancing in Leicester?"

"Forgive me," said Janice, "this idea was mine. You have to make some decisions quickly. There's no point in repeating the same old arguments. We invited Kylie along to see if the suggestion could work."

Kylie was looking at everyone in turn. "Can I say something? "she asked.

"Of course. Go ahead," said Philip.

"There seems to be two questions," she said. "Would you trust me to keep an eye on your mother and would Mrs Delgado and me get along, anyway. If she and I could get to know one another a little better, we might answer one of the questions."

"Sensible girl," said Victoria, "Let's leave these to argue amongst themselves and you can come with me to my own little home." She stood up and led the way. She moved like a dancer, Frank noted, she was light on her feet, balanced and elegant. Was she really older than he was?

"She's right," said Janice.

Left without the two principal players in the drama, they talked about the job offer, the accommodation which awaited, schools for the two sons. It was clear that, free of the responsibility of caring for Victoria, their immediate future could be rewarding. Frank and Janice gave glowing accounts of Kylie and her children.

"Oh dear!" Janice exclaimed, "We shall have to collect the children in ten minutes!"

Maria walked to the door which connected to the granny flat. She knocked before opening. A gale of laughter came out as Kylie and Victoria shared a joke.

"Bring the children back here," said Philip. "It would be good to meet them."

"I'll come with you," said Victoria, "it's only five minutes' walk."

Half an hour later the six adults had been joined by Emma, Ollie and the two Vallings boys, aged eleven and twelve. What had begun as a curious business meeting became a party.

"Whatever decision they come to," Victoria said as she bade goodbye to Kylie, "I want to see you again."

"Kyle," Philip said, "I hope you'll understand if we don't make a firm decision tonight. It has been an enjoyable afternoon, and it's clear that you and Victoria hit it off, but it is a very important decision."

Frank and Kylie walked home with the children Janice made her own way back.

Late the following morning Frank had a phone call from Philip Vallings. Philip had formally accepted the post in Leicester and he and Maria would be happy for Kylie to move into Pittsburg Street in one month's time. That would give the Vallings time to get the boys into new schools. Philip had no phone number for Kylie; would Frank please break the news and put her in touch?

After so many months sharing his big house, the prospect of being on his own once more was daunting. It meant another very big change in his life. He was not at all sure he was going to enjoy it.

Chapter fourteen

Poppy finished checking the fastenings on Oscar's seat. Martin was already behind the wheel. Poppy closed the rear door and half-turned towards her father.

"I can't believe I'll never see the place again," she said. There were tears in her eyes.

"It's the end of a chapter," said Frank. "We must get on with the rest of our lives." He paused and looked with her at the stone frontage, the windows and door frames which he painted several times in the past thirty years. "Yes, the old place holds lots of good memories and one or two sad ones. Best to think of the future."

She put her arms round him in one long, tearful embrace, then pulled away and climbed into the passenger seat beside her husband. She waved goodbye through the open window as the wheels crunched on the gravel. Frank watched as the car paused at the gate and turned left into the lane. His shoulders slumped a little and he turned back inside. His footsteps echoed in the empty hall as he made his way past cardboard boxes to the kitchen. He had left out what he needed to make tea but he did not want to stay inside. He took a mug of tea out into the garden. Instinctively he headed towards the far end, but he stopped short at the seat near the first apple tree, reminded by the sound of machinery of the work going on in the big field. Bulldozers and earth-moving vehicles were busy. Soon, he knew, the rustic fence he had built beyond the trees, the vegetable patch and the compost bins would all be crushed under the great metal tracks. The trees would go next. Soon after that the house itself, the house which had witnessed years of love and labour, joy and sadness would probably end up as hardcore for the access road.

But he no longer felt the same deep dismay. Life had moved on. He had made his decision three years ago now, prompted in the end by the information that the field was to be developed as an estate of more than thirty houses. His own property would be hemmed in after all these years. He had made enquiries and found the house was of less interest to estate agents than was his beloved garden. No one, he was told, would want to buy an old house with five bedrooms.

Despite all the work he had put into the place to make it comfortable, much more was needed to bring it up to modern standards with such matters as better insulation. If he played his cards right, he was told, the company that planned the new estate would pay a great deal of money to incorporate the old house and the garden into the new development. The suggested figure was mind-boggling. Now the time had come to leave.

It was quite irrational, Frank told himself, that the deep and painful regret he continued to feel was not for the loss of the house. That had served its purpose and no longer provided a truly appropriate place for one elderly man. Strictly speaking it had always been too big, even for a family of just three. A smaller house would have been better from the moment he and Louise were forced to accept Poppy would never have brothers or sisters. No, what grieved Frank far more was the loss of his garden and more especially the trees. He left his mug on the bench and walked slowly round the orchard, touching each familiar trunk like a lover. It was indeed irrational but the grief was stronger than he could control. It was only when he realised that the mechanical noises had ended and the light was fading that he turned back to the house, the upper windows reflecting the red sky. In the morning he would hand over the keys and drive away like Poppy for the last time. He had already dug up the most important rose which he had planted to commemorate Louise nearly five years ago.

There was little to keep him here now. Poppy and Martin, soon expecting a second child, were getting along with their lives. Janice had taken early retirement, her husband terminally ill. Jack and Iris were talking seriously of selling up and negotiating the purchase of a smaller property near their eldest son. Kylie had continued to clean the house two days each week, but had to fit her visits round her job in the school canteen during term time. He would miss her, but not as much as the children, now eleven and thirteen. Maybe they might be allowed to visit him in his new home. Kylie remained single, though Victoria had interested her in a dance group through which she had found other hobbies. and friends.

He was still fit and active and determined to begin the next part of his life energetically. He had enlisted numerous people to help him. Forty years' work with the Borough would provide a reasonable pension which, together with his state pension, would be enough for his day-to-day expenses. The handsome payment for the property was enough to buy an old building, complete with a large storage shed and even a modest patch of garden. When he had walked into the estate agents' office in Oakmere, he had been surprised to find the manager was Primrose. It made negotiations much easier than expected. The men's shed group had proved very helpful. The idea of relocating to Oakmere had taken firm root, although Primrose had been taken aback by the kind of property Frank wanted. About half a mile from the town centre there was a derelict, Methodist chapel, complete with its Sunday School building, rented for the moment to a local farmer. It was just what Frank wanted, to Primrose's astonishment. Water and electricity were available, though the main building was not habitable.

"It wouldn't cost all that much to convert it," Frank observed. "The main structure looks sound enough. I would want vacant possession, though, including the Sunday School."

He was in no rush. He had a structural engineer check the place out and an architect drew up plans. The Chapel would provide a comfortable cottage, centrally heated, with two bedrooms and a well-appointed living space with an almost professional kitchen. The farmer gave up the lease on his barn and Frank persuaded him to rent a small part of the adjoining field to turn into a decent garden, complete with a greenhouse. The Sunday school was needed, Frank explained, to store his horticultural equipment. Although his income would be adequate, his intention was to work as a jobbing gardener.

"Don't you want to retire properly?" asked Poppy.

"I'd be bored. There are always plenty of people wanting help with their gardens and this way I can do as much or as little as I like. It'll keep me fit, too. It will also be a good way to get to know people."

"Are you getting everything done before you move?"

"No. That will be part of the fun. I'll buy a caravan to live in while I oversee the building. That will give me a second guest bedroom when I've moved into the Chapel. There'll be room for you and Martin and several children, don't worry."

Poppy smiled at him. She was not entirely sure he was doing the right thing, but she admired him.

He stayed at the Farmers Arms until the caravan was delivered, a large, well-equipped thing which he bought second-hand. It was surprisingly comfortable. He was a tidy person and the van was easy to keep clean. There was only a rudimentary kitchen, but he was content to wait for the new building, since it was made to his exact design. He had plenty to do supervising the refurbishment of the Chapel. His first priority was to work on the Sunday School. (He continued to refer to the two buildings as the Chapel and the Sunday School, finding the names amusing, though he did not know why.) He could not explain why he was keen to clear the empty space. He knew he wanted to widen the doorway to allow access for a set of gang-mowers on a trailer and he intended to garage his four-wheel-drive vehicle inside. The existing floor was wooden and he replaced it with concrete, thus it was his tools that were first out of storage. They required no more than one third of the floor space, but he was left with plenty of room for a workshop. It also proved very useful for the temporary storage of materials to be used in the Chapel.

Another member of the Men's Shed, Pat, proved to be a builder.

"I'm basically a carpenter," he told Frank, "But I sub-contract electrical and plumbing work if the job is big enough. I'll give you a quote."

Frank also asked the architect to suggest other builders. Pat's quote was not the cheapest, but it seemed reasonable and he invited Frank to take a look at two, fair-sized houses that he had refurbished. Frank liked what he saw and gave Pat the contract. The work went well. Pat was a little surprised that Frank wanted the Sunday School done first, but went along with the work cheerfully. When a large van arrived with the equipment to go into the Sunday School building, however, he realised Frank's intention.

Within weeks five house-owners had spoken to Frank as he did his shopping or visited the bank or filled up with petrol. They wanted to know if he was going to work as a gardener and what were his charges.

"Not for a few months," he said. "I'm still settling into the old Chapel. Perhaps in the spring."

There was a slight delay caused by the need for work on the drains which involved the water company. Otherwise, there was no hold-up except for August Bank Holiday.

"It's our wedding anniversary," said Pat, three weeks in advance. "She'd kill me if I worked that weekend."

Frank had been so enjoying the process that he had not noticed they had been working without a break. Nearly all the work was indoors so even rain affected them only marginally. He did not feel the need for a break personally, but he made himself a picnic and drove the short distance into town to make his way to the seat by the river. It was already in use by a woman. She had a pad open on her lap and was sketching in watercolours.

"Oh!" she said, as Frank hesitated, and she moved the little selection of colours from the seat and put it on the arm.

"Sorry," Frank said, "I don't want to disturb you," and he made to walk on. She stopped him and insisted he take a seat next to her. Her name was Susan Braithwaite. She had lived in Oakmere many years and had just retired from teaching at the local comprehensive.

"Art?" Frank guessed, looking at the sketch of the family of swans.

"Good heavens, no! Maths. Do you live here? I don't think I've ever seen you."

Frank explained and found himself talking about his purchase of the old Chapel and his plan to become a jobbing gardener.

"Is the intention to turn your hobby into a way to earn money?" she asked.

"Not exactly."

"I assume gardening is your hobby."

Frank laughed. Susan was puzzled by his reaction and he explained further. She was impressed.

"I'm a keen amateur gardener myself," she said. "I might well make use of your expertise. Would you be able to prune tall hedges and fruit trees, that sort of thing?"

"No problem," he said, "but I want to get settled in first. I hope to start properly in the spring, but it depends what plants you want pruning. Some need to be done in the autumn and winter."

"Why don't you pop in and look for yourself?"

"OK."

Susan was interested in his plans for the Chapel. It had lain derelict for too long, she said. Was he planning to turn it into a shop? No, he told her, it would be his home and he did not intend to work full-time.

When she picked up her bag and put away the fresh sketch, now dry, they had been chatting for an hour. Frank said he would call her on the number she gave him. She stood up and they shook hands before she walked away towards the town.

Oakmere was not a tourist town. All the shops were closed, except for the supermarket. Frank bought the ingredients to make a curry before heading back to the caravan. A small cement mixer was the only outward sign that work was going on. Much of the structural work had been completed, including a staircase and a floor which extended over half the space. Stud walls would turn this space into two bedrooms and a bathroom. The ground floor as yet was no more than an open workshop. The main door was in the gable end, and would lead into a small entrance hall from where the stairs led upwards. A cloakroom and toilet led off the hall. The rest of this floor, the workshop, would be one, large, open space with a well-equipped kitchen and a comfortable, seating and dining area.

Frank set out the food and began the curry. When it was bubbling gently on the gas, he called Poppy.

"Just checking in," he said. "How are you all?"

"Everything's fine. What have you been up to? I hope you're not regretting the move. We worry about you on your own."

"You should know better than that," he said. "I've told you often enough, I'm used to being alone. And I haven't been stuck in here all day. I went into town and met a local and had a chat. She looks like being my first client."

"She?"

Frank laughed. "Don't jump to conclusions," he said. "I have no romantic ideas. I really don't want that kind of entanglement. I'm looking forward to a future life here once the Chapel is finished, and it's coming along nicely."

"I can't wait to see it."

"I shall want your help with that," Frank said, "I'm planning a housewarming party in late September."

"What kind of help? It's quite a long way to come. Don't forget I'm pregnant."

"Nothing too strenuous. Just keep the last two weeks of September free. I'll sort it out with you later. Must go before my dinner's spoiled."

He hung on long enough for Oscar to say hello and goodbye, then served up his curry. He had bought some Naan bread, but it was not as good as his own cooking. It would be great to take possession of the new kitchen.

He continued to join the men's shed group every Thursday, but once he was living in or at least very close to Oakmere, his relationship with the other men changed. He had already consulted Steve professionally. Now he dealt with Primrose and Pat. Pat proved an excellent tradesman. The work progressed on time and with good humour. Other members of the men's shed took an interest and expected a progress report every Thursday. The change in relationship came about by dealing with individuals away from the weekly meetings. And, while Frank found the information and local knowledge valuable, his new friends also showed interest in his own expertise. Two or three of them were themselves keen gardeners. They invited Frank to look at their gardens and to suggest improvements. Several also dropped in unexpectedly to see for themselves how the work was progressing. By September Frank had become part of a friendly network. Any remaining fears Poppy might have that her father might be lonely were quite wrong.

The kitchen arrived in October. Frank's first reaction was a mixture of excitement and anxiety. There appeared to be far too many appliances and cupboards. Still wrapped in their protective plastic, they took up most of the floor space.

"Don't worry," Pat advised with a smile, "once it's all in place, you'll be surprised."

It all went together quickly. Frank felt like a small boy at Christmas, able to guess the contents of each wrapped parcel, but forced to wait to touch them. The last two or three days were the worst, as he watched Pat and his mate fix the tiles on the wall and grout them. At last, they gave the tiles a polish, removed the cover from the work surface and cleaned it before cleaning the floor. The result was spectacular and magnificent.

"I don't really understand," Pat said, hands on hips as he looked at his handiwork, "why you wanted all this equipment. It's not as though you're going to cook for a big family."

"All my life I've wanted a kitchen like this," Frank explained. "I'm a keen cook."

Pat smiled and shrugged. "It's your choice, I suppose. It is pretty impressive, I admit."

"I'll give it a good workout very soon," Frank promised.

He had already told everyone to make themselves available for the housewarming. Poppy and Martin travelled down two days in advance with Oscar and were accommodated in the caravan, while he moved into his new bedroom. Poppy was seven months pregnant but Frank knew she would want to help with the preparations. He planned an ambitious buffet, most of which he prepared in the days before. There was plenty of room in the new fridge-freezer.

Poppy was astonished by the numbers. The entire men's shed was invited, together with wives or partners and children. They were catering for about forty-five people; Frank told his daughter.

The party was a huge success. The day before, Poppy and Oscar inflated lots of balloons and attached them to the gate. They also made a lot of bunting which Martin hung around the small square made by the Chapel, the Sunday School, and the caravan. In the spring, Frank explained, there would be room for a vegetable plot nearby. Meanwhile the Sunday School had been cleaned and tidied. Frank's vehicle and equipment, such as ladders, medium-sized mowers, chain saw and very clean hand tools of all kinds, was stored there, leaving sufficient space at one end for a sturdy work bench.

The farmer who had previously rented the Sunday School, had provided a dozen straw bales for seating. He would take them away after the party and use them as bedding for his animals.

"The food was very good," Martin observed, the day after the event. "It was truly professional."

"You are a clever old thing," Poppy said. "What happens to all the left-over bits? I've put them in two plastic buckets."

"Porky is calling for them later."

"Who is Porky?"

"The pig farmer."

"Ah! What about all the paper plates and stuff?"

"We'll take that to the recycling centre tomorrow."

Martin, Poppy, and Frank had begun clearing up, but were surprised when Pat arrived.

"Thought you could do with a hand," he said.

By lunchtime most of the work was done. There was plenty of food left over for a quick snack. Frank thanked Pat before he drove home.

"That was a great party," Pat said. "And I'm glad you like the conversion."

He left.

"I think I'll take a nap," said Poppy, tapping her swollen belly. "You two can look after Oscar for an hour." She went over to the caravan and closed the door behind her. Oscar, it seemed, was also tired. He did not want to play games but curled up in a large armchair and fell asleep. The two men sat and chatted.

"It's amazing," Martin said. "You seem to have made lots of friends already. Poppy was worried when you decided to move after so long. It's working out well, though."

"It's partly down to you."

"To me? Why on earth do you say that?"

"You won't remember, but you pointed out that the old house would be worth good money. 'A small fortune' I think you said."

"Oh, did I?"

"You were right. The place was too big. I knew that, but it held so many memories."

"No regrets?"

"No, not now." They fell silent for a while. Oscar was asleep as only a child can sleep, totally at peace.

"I'm not entirely sure what comes next," Frank said.

"I thought you were going back to gardening."

"Well, yes, but this place offers other possibilities."

"Hang on," Martin said. "You're supposed to be retired."

Frank laughed. "I know," he said, "but all this is too much for me to enjoy on my own."

Martin gave him a sharp look. "Have you got someone in mind?"

"No, no! Don't misunderstand me. It's only a vague idea as yet."

"Another plan?"

"Look," Frank said, "I'm going to look around for charities. I suppose my experience with Kylie sparked this off. There must be lots of single parents living on the breadline who simply can't afford to take their children on holiday."

"I suppose there are."

"Well, I've now got an empty caravan, once you and Poppy and Oscar here have gone back home. I'm thinking, with a very small contribution, once I've got my garden up and growing, it would cost me next to nothing to offer accommodation with vegetarian meals thrown in. It would also give me a real excuse for all the extravagance." He pointed at the gleaming kitchen.

Martin gaped. "You never cease to astonish me," he said.

After a while Frank said, "I sometimes think time is like a river."

"Eh?"

"We're a bit like swans. Time carries us along like the birds. Sometimes we grab the branch of a tree as we float past, but we have to let go in the end."

"Are you talking about your search for your father?"

"That was more like paddling against the current."

"Very poetic. I'm not sure it works too well as a metaphor"

Frank smiled. "There was no way I could ever get back to the source," he said. "It meant paddling against the current and I was being carried further and further away

"So, you've given up?"

"Yes, I've given up. What do they say? Go with the flow? We can't go back, only forwards. Sooner or later, you have to let go."

Martin looked at his father-in-law. Frank was facing the window but he was not looking at anything. His expression suggested he was in a dream, possibly replaying some of the many memories that were his and his alone. He looked a little sad, or maybe he was simply tired. He was, after all, sixty-six years old. He said he had let go, but it was as though he was floating on that river but facing backwards much of the time, upstream. He was reconciled to the irresistible stream maybe, but his thoughts were of the past at this moment.

They sat there in the silent, old Chapel, with the child sleeping nearby, until Frank suddenly stood up.

"Time for a decent cup of tea," he announced, and ran a loving hand along his worktop before opening a cupboard door.

THE END

Milton Keynes UK
Ingram Content Group UK Ltd.
UKHW030158010324
438680UK00001B/12